DICKIE

DICKIE

A Novel

WAYNE TEFS

First published in 1993 by
House of Anansi Press Limited
1800 Steeles Avenue West
Concord, Ontario
L4K 2P3
(416) 445-3333

Canadian Cataloguing in Publication Data

Tefs, Wayne, 1947-
Dickie

ISBN 0-88784-537-1

I. Title.

PS8589.E37D52 1993   C813'.54   C93-093589-6
PR9199.3.T44D52   1993

Cover Design Concept: Angel Guerra
Cover Design: Brant Cowie/ArtPlus Limited
Cover Photograph: Michael Tindal
Typesetting: Tony Gordon Limited
Printed and bound in Canada

*House of Anansi Press gratefully acknowledges the support of the Canada
Council, The Ontario Ministry of Culture, Tourism, and Recreation,
Ontario Arts Council, and Ontario Publishing Centre in the development of
writing and publishing in Canada.*

For my mother, Stella,
and my father, Armin,
and my sisters,
Sharon and Kelly

Acknowledgments: thanks to Alison Gillmor,
Mark Duncan, Michael Davis,
and Kristen Wittman;
special thanks to Dennis and Dave.

he climbs up on my knee
he means the world to me
to me he'll always be
that little boy of mine

— traditional song

One

My brother, Ralph, first tried to kill himself in the same year the Russians put a satellite into space. 1957, was it? The year Father began downing a bottle of whiskey every night, the year Mother found out what was behind the dizzy spells making her vomit every morning — of which, more later. The year I turned fifteen and Ralph, about to graduate from Red Rock High, seventeen. What a year. Here are some of the other things that happened: Ralph and I visited High Park in Toronto, he held a loaded Luger to my head, and we succumbed to the seductive charms of Lola and the Dancing Damselles of Denmark.

But I get ahead of myself. First came Werner von Braun and the magic of science. Yes, *the* Werner von Braun right in Red Rock High, the man they called the Führer behind his back, the brains that landed a man on the moon within ten short years! Twelve, actually.

He had been whisked out of Germany, before the collapse of the Third Reich, by the invading American forces to work on their rocket program. And there he was a decade later in Red Rock, telling us about the wonders of the atom in his clipped English and clicking his heels on the stage and dipping in a ridiculous Nazi bow when we rose as one to give him a thunderous round of applause. He was graying around the temples. He wore a bow tie. He had come to Red Rock, he told us, because he had to tell us about entropy and space-time. He demonstrated with a Möbius strip, he explained about the Klein bottle. As he spoke, he held both arms out front the way evangelical preachers do. He told anecdotes, he joked, he charmed the pants off us. Yes, he was an inspiration.

But he had an ulterior motive for being in our town. Unknown to us, he had come on a scouting mission to have a look at the wunderkind of Red Rock High, my brother Ralph, who scored perfect results on NASA's tests for spotting young geniuses.

Oh Werner, the rockets of desire you ignited in one breast!

At home that night Ralph's eyes shone with tears of joy. He'd spent an hour after school talking to the great man himself. I'd been waiting for him, tossing an Indian rubber ball against the garage door and practicing my fielding. "It's so easy," he explained, "just break the Earth's gravitational belt and WHOOSH — " He was talking about putting a man into orbit around the Earth, and as he spoke his face flushed.

We leaned over the dining-room table and he showed me on a piece of paper, drawing the Earth as a ball and circling it with a narrow band he shaded in with pencil. That was the Earth's gravitational field. Beyond, the uncharted where von Braun was determined to go. "Just think, Dickie," Ralph whispered to me, "man's going to conquer space." He dragged me to the doorstep by the elbow. He looked to the heavens and pointed straight up with one thin arm. "And I'll be there when we do it. Me, Ralph Bascom Frudel." He picked up his rough diagram and rushed off to tell Matt Stockton about Werner von Braun, about solid fuels, about alloys, about God knows what mysteries of space travel.

That was September of the year Ralph was in grade twelve — in but not of, since he studied physics and maths and chemistry on his own, two years ahead of everyone else. Within weeks came a letter from von Braun's office in Alabama, a letter such as we'd never seen before in Red Rock, where the road the Royal Mail truck traveled from Port Arthur was one track of asphalt running through the granite hills. This letter came in a cream envelope with gold embossed letters reading Office Of The Director NASA. And inside, cream paper thick to the touch, more gold lettering on the heading, von Braun's personal signature, a flourish of thick blue ink at the bottom, words inviting Ralph to the California Institute of Technology.

My lord. A summons from the gods themselves would have stirred less excitement in our modest bungalow, around our mining town where Saturday's entertainment was running through the iron-red roads and Sunday's respite picking blueberries in the mosquito-thick shrub-tangled hills. Ralph's hands shook as he reread the letter, mouthing each word. "Look, Dickie," he said, and bestowed on me the singular honor of reading it next. "And all Dad has to pay is tuition." He showed it to the whole neighborhood — and even Mrs. Valencourt who hated us kids for throwing tomatoes at her house and shook her fist at us and called us young buggers stood at the end of her driveway to read it and smiled in a self-congratulatory way. Even Mrs. V.

Then it was off to the principal's for tea. Mother insisted we both go, arguing Ralph should have moral support (and secretly hoping, I know now, the heady atmosphere of serious talk, of learning, might rub off on me, the younger, the less-able brother). We scrubbed our faces and Mother patted our hair with tonic and helped us into blue blazers before Father drove us to Prungle's on the far side of town. Houses with paved drives and bedrooms upstairs. Mrs. Prungle met us at the door. I smelled something wonderful about her immediately, the scent of flowers. She wore a print dress with a scooped neck and sandals, her painted nails peeked out of them. I was instantly in love, though I didn't know it right away. While we exchanged pleasantries at the door I rubbed my thumbs and forefingers together, worrying skin off both.

Seated in the living room were Mr. Rook, who taught Ralph physics, and Dr. Mendez, who everybody called Badger because of his protruding front teeth, from math. They shook Ralph's hand and beamed proudly over the glasses of punch Mrs. Prungle ladled from a crystal bowl.

I made two blunders there:

I drank my punch too fast,

I kept staring at Mrs. Prungle's neckline.

What a clod. Everyone noticed but I was saved embarrassment by Badger Mendez, who treated us to a disquisition on the properties of the ionosphere, was it? Let's say.

"Not at all," said Mr. Rook when Badger was done, and countered with gas rings around the sun. Blah blah entropy, blah blah black holes. They rose to go to the back porch and study gas rings or some such thing, and Mrs. Prungle and I were left alone with the punch. She poured me another glass.

She asked, "And are you another budding scientist?"

I was, if anything, an indifferent athlete, my size being an advantage on the football field, where I'd made the varsity team even though I was only in grade ten. I could hardly tell Mrs. Prungle that. Anyway, my face was hot, my hands clammy. I had no idea what to say but even if I'd had, no words would have come from my constricted throat. I picked at the crease in my flannel trousers. I shrugged my shoulders in the way of younger brothers and tried not to look too dumb, and then Mrs. Prungle offered me more punch and a photo album of Toronto where she'd lived as a girl. She sat beside me on the couch. Was it face powder I smelled? My heart raced.

We looked at photos of Queen's Park, which I knew Mrs. Prungle must have liked because besides the copper-green statues of men on horses there was a profusion of flowers: peonies, tiger lilies, many whose names Mrs. Prungle told me and I instantly forgot. Then we looked at the Island ferry with Mr. Prungle waving from the upper deck, a stupid grin on his idiotic face. Exhibition Stadium with its thousands of seats, Maple Leaf Gardens, the Public Baths. We lingered over Kensington Market: chickens hanging from their yellow feet, fish on great slabs of blue ice, dark-skinned faces, orange dresses, red hats, a man with a gold ring through his nose. And the stone buildings at the University of Toronto: they caught light as they climbed into the blue sky, the green ivy matted to their walls. Mrs. Prungle leaned over to point it out, her breath hot on my cheek. By the time Mr. Prungle brought the group back from the porch I was crazy in love and I was mad to visit that great city.

4

But it was time to go home.

I shook Mr. Prungle's hand and looked into Mrs. Prungle's eyes, but not a word would croak past my thick tongue. I stumbled down the sidewalk, dazed.

In the car Badger Mendez talked about California. "There's beaches for miles and miles." He laughed. "And sand. Miles of it, and so fine it squeaks under your heel." He looked into the back seat at me and smiled his crooked smile. Ralph would love California because it was so warm and so beautiful. Didn't Ralph play tennis? The perfect climate for tennis. And the perfect place for a young man with ambitions. In California everyone was like Ralph — smart, talented, keen. They lived the American Dream. They were in love with traveling space as well as with space travel, he said, making a teacher's joke, yuk yuk. In California they had mountains where Red Rock had slag heaps, and crashing surf where we had mosquitoes, static, and grime. "And the oranges," Badger suddenly blurted out, "I almost forgot about the oranges. They grow right on the trees in your yard and you pick them for breakfast." When he dropped us off he ruffled my hair in an avuncular way and shook Ralph's hand for a long time.

Lord we were happy that day. I was in love with Mrs. Prungle, Ralph with his future — including the red Mercedes with wing doors, he'd gone on about it forever it seemed. Everybody was talking about breaking the sound barrier and rockets and space travel. The President had pledged an American would be first on the moon. Whatever it took, the President promised, we would win: brains, money, arm-twisting. Now Ralph would be part of that pledge, one of the people hand-picked by von Braun to take man to the moon and who knew where else. Part of the NASA team.

"I can't wait, Dickie," my brother Ralph said. "Think of it — weightlessness, the ionosphere. And liquid fuels, you wouldn't believe what they're doing with liquid fuels. It's incredible, impossible, marvelous, and glorious. Shit."

He hugged me. He skipped across the lawn and did a back flip, blond hair rooster-tailing despite the Vitalis Mother had smoothed on it hours earlier. "I'll actually be part of it, me, me," Ralph shouted. "There's the letter, there's von Braun's signature."

He pulled the cream envelope from an inside pocket of his jacket and kissed it once, twice, three times. He seized my hands. We jigged in the yard, we danced around the spruces Father and I had planted along the driveway in the spring. Then Ralph lay down on the grass and spread-eagled himself to the sky. "Take me," he called to the sun, "take me kun flamo, kun varmo, kun deziro."

"Get off it," I said, referring to the words Ralph was speaking.

They were Esperanto, of course. They meant *with flame, with heat, with passion.*

Ralph was fond of Esperanto, the so-called international language, created and promoted by Dr. L. L. Zamenhof in the late nineteenth century as an antidote to the stupidities of his time and all others — prejudice, parochialism, racism — things Lazar Ludovik Zamenhof, a Polish Jew, knew well and called the "ancient enemies of mankind." Of which an example later. Such stupidities, according to Zamenhof, were behind wars such as the Great War in Europe — eight million dead and sixteen million wounded, not to mention slaughter, mayhem, madness, and reparations.

Esperanto was meant to change all that. According to Zamenhof, "the multiplicity of languages is the chief cause dividing human beings and making of them unfriendly units." Zamenhof believed all men are brothers, "ke ciuj homoj estas fratoj." He was an idealist and he set out to change the world by developing one language for all peoples to speak. For Zamenhof, a common world language was the most important means of abolishing misunderstandings and hatreds among the peoples of the world and creating mutual understanding and respect.

This was so much gobbledegook as far as Ralph was concerned, but he had an Esperanto saying on a piece of Bristol board tacked above his bed. He was a document in contradiction. "Una nova mondo de paco kaj amo," it read. A new world of peace and love.

I believed in that, too. In the ninth grade I'd joined the United Nations Club where we read the speeches of Woodrow Wilson and Dag Hammarskjöld and held mock debates about the armed conflict in Korea and about Red China's right to membership in the U.N. When the Suez Crisis broke out, our staff adviser, Miss Crawford, cautioned us not to take sides, even though the *Winnipeg Free Press* blatantly favored the position of British prime minister Anthony Eden. But when our own Lester Pearson made the speech proposing peace-keeping forces, we listened round a transistor radio in Miss Crawford's classroom and cheered when the motion passed.

Ralph did not belong to the United Nations Club. But at home we listened to the news at six o'clock on the CBC, and he said to me, "Today, Dickie, Canada has its first statesman, today the eyes of the world are on us. Granda Lester, vi salutas." We raised our glasses of milk in a toast and Ralph added, "Excessive, but a little excess never hurt, right, mia frato?"

Esperanto itself means "one who is hoping or hopeful," from the root *esperi*, to hope, and the first book of the "internacio lingvo" was coyly published under the name *Dr. Esperanto*. Ralph told me that the proponents of Esperanto are hopeful about the fate of the human race. Hopeful about the destiny of a species capable of slaughtering millions of its fellows twice within a thirty-year span. And hopeful, too, that mankind will not only survive but flourish. They believe in the power of language to bridge national differences and international misunderstanding. The Esperanto movement, Ralph said, is utopian, utilitarian, idealist, visionary, and naive. Imagine setting out to solve the problems of the world by creating a language!

Esperanto, then, the language of brotherhood, of peace, the language of love. Lingvo de amo. Is that why my brother Ralph had taken to studying it, to memorizing its polyglot nouns and verbs? Flamo for flame, folio for leaf, gorgo for throat, dikfingro for thumb? He threw these words at me and gave me his Groucho Marx wink when Mother looked puzzled and Father exclaimed *talk English for petessake*. He confided to me he thought Esperanto would be the language of science and commerce by the year 2000 and he wanted to be in on that, on the cutting edge. I suspected, though, his real reason for learning it was to fool our parents.

"Dickie," Ralph whispered to me, "we know latko means milk, but what is the word for whiskey?" By this time it was evening and we were in his room, sitting on the bed, Ralph reclining on the pillows, his favorite position, wearing a white T-shirt like Marlon Brando. He had his feet crossed out front. One elbow rested on a stack of comics, and Ralph held a *Playboy* on his lap, which he flipped through as we talked. Did I say he was handsome in a roguish way? Did I say he had a brown spot in one of his blue eyes everyone who met him was fixated by?

"You see," he said, "if we know the language of booze, then we'll be able to talk about drinking and they won't know. Hodiaunokt trinkos viskio," he said. "Jes? Tre bona, Dickie, mia frato. Tre bona."

He was talking about whiskey but he was drunk on words.

Two

Hansi Frudel drank, too, but he was not yet spending every evening downing enough whiskey to knock himself out before bed. That would come later.

Hansi wasn't a drinker. But on hot summer days he'd have a cold beer with supper. And he was no puritan. He'd let his boys share one, Dickie sipping from a glass, Ralph tipping the bottle back, smacking his lips loudly and saying "granda, tre granda." And Saturdays when Hansi took Tina dancing at the Legion Hall he sipped beer between polkas to slake his thirst. Two-Bottle Hansi his friends called him. As a rule that's all he drank.

So on nights that fall of 1957 when Ralph was seventeen and Hansi sat in the kitchen, elbows on the table, a pad of lined paper in front of him filled with columns of numbers, he had no need of a water tumbler full of rye. He was calculating how to cover Ralph's tuition to Cal Tech. But he had not yet begun to mutter to himself in a hoarse half whisper, *Hansi, Hansi.*

"Hansi" was a diminutive of Handel. Hansi's mother had had great hopes for her three sons. The eldest she named Emmanuel and the youngest Friedrich. She claimed they descended from a cousin of the great Bismarck, a cousin who'd been spirited out of Germany for incurring the Kaiser's wrath during the Franco-Prussian wars. About what she didn't know. Yet she told her sons and then her grandsons, "The blood of von Bismarck flows through your veins, the blood of great men."

To Hansi she gave a ring with a large crimson stone: the sole treasure the cousin had been able to get out of Germany in his flight from the tyrannical Kaiser. Hansi wore it on his pinky finger, and at least once a day he stopped and turned it to the sun, admiring the way it caught light as he revolved his hand. The gold was worn smooth near the stone. Held to the light, the stone glinted like a drop of dark blood, suggesting deep and dark secrets.

Hansi and his brothers were ambitious. Emmanuel went to the seminary in Minneapolis, and Friedrich to study languages at the university. Hansi enrolled in business school. Everyone was just getting started when events in the larger world intervened. First the Depression came, forcing the seminary in Minneapolis to close. Emmanuel returned and settled in as a school teacher. It was around then that Hansi married Tina, and Ralph was born when Hitler invaded Poland. Hansi and Friedrich enlisted in the infantry, wanting to show they were Canadians and would fight the enemies of democracy wherever they sprang up. Before Hansi got his orders to ship overseas, Tina was pregnant again. Friedrich died on the Normandy beaches along with thousands of young Canadians, and Hansi fought in Italy. When he returned home he had a heart full of sad memories and a family to care for.

He started up one business after another. Hansi's Hot Foods was a stand specializing in frankfurters and potato chips. After three years he sold the stand and put the profits into property. He bought building lots in Fort Garry and sold them once the city installed sewer and water systems. He turned a quick dollar there and moved into real estate, selling houses to war veterans. When he'd accumulated enough cash, he bought a corner garage and pumped gas for a year. Ralph was in school by then, Dickie was four. Then came a café in the trucker's end of town where he served sandwiches and pie with ice cream. All Hansi's business ventures were successful, but none really profitable. He was still waiting to make it big, as he said, when Tina became pregnant again, and that's when they moved to Red Rock.

Hansi had had his eye on Red Rock for years. An iron-mining town, it had doubled in population between V-E Day and the outbreak of war in Korea, and then doubled again in just two years. What did the burgeoning postwar economy need more than raw iron to make steel for cars, refrigerators, stoves, and the thousand construction projects put off during the war? "And look at the wages those miners make," Hansi said to Tina over the kitchen table. "Three bucks an hour. Starting!" He knew miners were easy come easy go with money, and he had ideas about helping them spend some of it.

Tina had questions. "What about schools?"

Of course there were schools, Hansi pointed out. And new ones, too, because the town was new. Smart brick buildings filled with young teachers, not the doddering old women like at Sir George Grammar where Ralph and Dickie went. Miss Payne, Miss Neal.

Tina asked, "What about living with miners and miners' kids?" She'd read bad things about Red Rock. Wildcat strikes. Street fights. A year earlier a miner had come home from graveyard shift and found his wife with another man: he'd killed them both with a shotgun right in the bed. The photos in the papers showed bloody sheets and half-naked bodies. It was okay for men to go to places like Red Rock and earn big money, Tina thought, but what about raising a family there? Among transients, toughs, immigrants, Catholics. Who would move to such a place?

"They're ordinary people," Hansi argued, thinking perhaps of the men he'd fought beside in Italy. Sons of farmers, miners, and fishermen. "Just like you and me, Tina. It won't be so bad. In fact, it'll be good with all the fresh air and open space for the boys to run around in."

"And bears. And mosquitoes. And toughs. Prostitutes."

"Tina."

"These towns springing out of the rocks. There's too much money around and too little to do. And the men who work there have no roots, no commitments . . ."

"It won't be so bad."

And at first it wasn't so bad. Because a businessman with Hansi's talents can make money in a mining town when he opens a retail store. Hansi's Hardware and Sporting Goods, the neon sign read. Benjamin Moore Paints. Spalding baseball gloves. Fishing tackle and fresh minnows. All the miners bought rifles at moose hunting season, and on rifles Hansi cleared twenty-five dollars.

He hired a stock clerk and ran the cash register up front himself, talking to the miners about fishing and local politics as he wrapped their purchases in brown paper. The miners were all union men who had little time for politicians or entrepreneurs like C. D. Howe and K. C. Irving. Behind his back they laughed at Hansi, too, at his capitalist ambitions, at his accent — some of them even called him Krauthead, having heard him talk about battles in Italy and misunderstanding which side he'd been on. But generally he was well enough liked. When they came through the door the men who knew Hansi mimicked his favorite saying: *Have I got a deal for you!* But they slapped him on the back to show they were only teasing.

"Best prices in town."

"Yes, Hansi. Of course, Hansi."

"Look." He dragged down a catalogue and opened it to fishing reels, pointing out that in Toronto the new stock was priced at seven dollars and he sold Shakespeare reels for six. "I'm not making a lot of money, see. At less than six dollars I might as well be giving them away."

"All right, Hansi. Sold. Wrap one up. Two."

It was said by those who knew him that Hansi enjoyed the sport of making sales more than the profits he earned by them. There was some truth in that remark, because he never made a lot of money. Even when the boom was at its peak and the mines worked around the clock, paying Red Rock's miners the highest wages in the country, he made just enough to cover his mortgages and take his family on a short vacation to Winnipeg every summer. Those were the good years just after the war when America's steel mills couldn't get enough raw iron, and even the Germans, friends now under the Marshall Plan, were placing orders for Red Rock hematite. There were three open pit mines in production then, and the men arriving from Northern Ontario, Quebec, and British Columbia to toil in the red clay went straight to Hansi's for boots and hard hats.

At the height of the boom two more hardware stores opened, Fred's, on the far side of town, and a branch of the Beaver Lumber chain at the opposite end of Main Street from Hansi's. No one wondered then what would happen if the mines stopped production and laid men off because then everyone was too busy placing orders to think about the future. Out the door of Hansi's went paint, hammers, nails, posthole augers, spades, rakes, lawn seed, ladders, door locks, wood screws, shotguns — and in came dollars, dollars, dollars. It was the boom and the boom mentality: Hula Hoops, Wiffle balls, Fizzies. The Stocktons bought a freezer at Eaton's and the Alexas a TV: "Zorro," "American Bandstand," "Queen for a Day."

A new Safeway went up on the vacant lot next to Hansi's and branches of the Bank of Montreal and Toronto-Dominion farther down the street. More construction workers needing boots and lunch pails: more orders for cement, rivets, shingles, wire. Hansi hired a clerk and knocked down the wall in back to increase storage space. Widened the front door, ordered a second neon sign. And took another mortgage to finance these renovations. Thirty thousand dollars riding on his signature.

That was in the early fifties. When he wasn't busy at the cash register or shifting inventory with Hopeless Mike — so slow he was the only man in Red Rock fired from the mines in a decade — Hansi stood at the door, hands in apron, and marveled at the construction on Main Street. With the Rockland Hotel and Woolworth's, Red Rock was becoming a real city. Sidewalks, fresh asphalt, streetlights, dance clubs, hookers. Already there were ten thousand people in town. In five, ten years, who knew? There was talk of building a highway through the muskeg and granite of the Laurentian Shield to Fort Frances and then on to Winnipeg.

And though the thought of mortgages sometimes crossed his mind like a black cloud — a note for thirty grand was nothing to sneeze at in the fifties — Hansi was not really worried. In those days, talk of expansion, of development filled the air. The Steep Rock mine had invested two million dollars in new Euclid earth haulers, and Caland Ore nearly as much in a dragline. McGuire, the manager at the Toronto-Dominion, had given Hansi assurances. And anyway, Hansi had given some thought to future disasters and put away some money: he had a trust account in Tina's name. Five thousand. Their house had cost less. So Hansi Frudel wasn't thinking gloomy thoughts or staring into the bottoms of whiskey glasses then.

Or having bad dreams.

Three

Tina Frudel had been having bad dreams for years. They'd started after she lost her child of several hours — her third — and had grown worse as time passed. These were nightmares, actually, phantasmagora scenes where bridge planking collapsed underfoot, sucking her screaming sons' hands from hers and plunging them into a swirling river, or where houses roared in flames while the boys cried at upstairs windows.

Whenever she dreamt this way, she awoke with a start. Beside her Hansi shifted and grunted. The first time she'd started awake from one of these nightmares — years ago — he'd rolled over and asked her what was wrong. She wept. She explained. Then he rubbed her temples the way she liked. And when she still couldn't fall asleep, he went into the kitchen and came back with a glass of whiskey. "To calm your nerves," he said.

It burned the back of Tina's throat, and for days she burped a sour taste of molasses. And it hadn't made her fall asleep. Instead she tossed until dawn and woke with a queasy stomach and a headache lasting all morning. And Hansi had tossed along with her. Near dawn he'd rolled over and sighed in an exasperated way. He had to be at the hardware store by seven. So after the first time when she woke with a start Tina lay rigid as an iron bar and stared at the ceiling, waiting to drop back into fitful sleep. Most times morning came and she was still staring at the ceiling.

But the dreams didn't stop.

And so Tina thought they were God's way of punishing her for letting her little girl die — which is how she thought of the baby's loss during the long nights when she studied the ceiling and listened to Hansi breathing beside her and felt her own heart pumping in her throat. The doctors said the baby died of too much fluid, that it drowned, really, in her womb.

There were three of them gathered round her bed at the hospital the day after the death. The young one asked, "Do you drink a lot?" He must have sensed Tina's reaction, the way her body went rigid, because he added quickly, "Studies show consumption during pregnancy — " But by this time Tina was in tears. A nonsmoker, a teetotaler, Tina Frudel was not the sort of woman to risk life, even unborn life. Silence fell around the white hospital bed as Tina sobbed and buried her face in the pillows. The doctors shrugged their shoulders and had no more questions for a woman who had just lost a baby.

And it had been such a beautiful baby: a girl with a shock of the blackest hair and big round eyes. She weighed exactly seven pounds. By now she would be ten years old. Her raven hair would fall to her shoulders and Tina would brush it out, making sparks fly and making both of them laugh, mother and daughter, laughing and crying and whispering together. Pals. This also Tina thought as she lay in the dark, blaming herself.

On Sundays she went to church, and sitting on the hard pew she prayed for two things: that God forgive her, and that He take away the nightmares. She was convinced they were sent to punish her, and this conviction went deep because Tina was nursing a guilty secret. When the doctors were busy hinting things about alcohol — and she was indignantly brushing them off — she'd neglected to mention that all through her pregnancy she drank coffee. Abnormal amounts, maybe. She always had a pot on the stove. From morning until bedtime she sipped at it as she worked about the house or sat with a friend. When they came by Tina always had a biscuit for them, and with their biscuit, mugs of coffee. It was the same at their places: cookies and coffee and chit-chat.

She hadn't remembered about the coffee right after the baby's death while she was feeling low and the doctors were pestering her with questions. But later she realized she *had* consumed a lot of fluid, if not the kind the doctors were thinking about. Because she'd brought their questions to an abrupt end, they'd never learned her secret. But in her heart Tina stood condemned. And she felt her sin so deeply she could not even share it with Hansi. She sealed her lips on the guilt, deciding to take it to the grave. Only she would ever know she was a murderer — and God.

Sometimes Hansi would find her in a room staring out a window. He would ask, "What is it?"

"Nothing," she would sigh. And then, "I was thinking about Ann-Marie." They had named the baby Ann-Marie and buried her in the cemetery at the edge of town: Pastors Sims with his Bible, her sons in blue blazers, gray flannels, and polished brogues.

"Ah," Hansi said softly. Ann-Marie was one of those subjects best left alone between people long married. He put his arm around her shoulder and stared out the window, too.

And in her heart Tina cursed the drinking of coffee. She was an even-tempered woman, but her mind turned pitch black when she thought of this. The day she made the connection between Ann-Marie's death and coffee, she threw the perculator in the trash and dumped all the ground coffee in the cupboards down the toilet. God damn you, she muttered as she flushed once and then a second time, while the grounds swirled in eddies of water and then were sucked down forever. It was the first time she'd sworn aloud. And God damn me, she added. I'm guilty but I stand here innocent as a new bride and Hansi knows nothing. He doesn't know I'm a killer.

She studied her face in the mirror and asked herself, *how can I be this way, how can God let me live?*

When the nightmares continued, she decided instead of trying to forget them she would punish herself, forcing them on her conscience the way she worked the tip of her tongue raw in a cavity until it bled. So she dwelt on the images that made her feel worst — and savored the feelings of guilt and remorse. Some mornings she sat at the kitchen table and wrote out her dreams, wallowing in shame and despair.

But the nightmares grew worse. Tina found herself in an alley beating her boys with a stick and laughing hideously. She woke with her arm twitching, feeling the heft of the stick in her hand. She decided she was not just a murderer, but a psychopath.

In church on Sunday morning she asked God how He could take the life of an innocent child and save a sadist like herself. She went about the house in a daze. At one time she'd spent her days listening to the radio — Don Messer and His Islanders, The Happy Gang, John Drainie. Now when the boys were at school she read magazine articles about madness, nodding knowingly over shared symptoms: vacant staring among them. She bought the tabloids and read and reread the pieces on psychopathic killers. She studied their psychological profiles, equating herself with women who strangled their babies or poisoned their parents. She called herself Tina the Terrible.

She came to believe she had murdered her baby, and that in some obscure way the child's innocent life had been sacrificed so she might live. In those moments she felt despair such as, she imagined, no one had ever experienced before. Sweat ran down her brow and she felt dizzy.

One day she was doing the dishes and suddenly gagged, vomit forcing its way past her mouth and dribbling into the dishwater. Every morning afterward she knelt over the toilet, each hand clutching the rim of cold porcelain while her gorge went into spasm and heaved up her breakfast. Sometimes there was blood, and always a stabbing pain at the base of her neck. *Tina, Tina,* she moaned. Though she suffered torment, she told herself it was the only way she would be cleansed of her sin, that she deserved to suffer in pain.

And this was before the doctors discovered the leukemia.

Four

It affected her that way because there was a streak of craziness in Mother's family. Her father was an old coot who went shopping at his local Safeway wearing a three-piece pin-striped suit but no shoes. An aunt was a reflexologist. That wasn't the worst. Two of our cousins committed suicide in their teens, one by shooting herself, the other by drowning. And my mother's younger brother, who suffered clinical depressions from the time he became deaf in one ear, was killed by a car on a country road. The coroner's report read death by accident, but the accident took place in broad daylight and the car was coming toward him. He was twenty-six.

The day that happened we were sitting at the kitchen table for lunch, Ralph and I home from school, Mother ladling soup while the radio buzzed John Drainie's "Story Time" behind our noontime chatter. When the telephone rang, Mother turned down the radio. Then followed the kind of silence when you hear birds chirping in the yard out back, the hum of electric clocks. "Dickie," Mother whispered past her hand, "run to the store and get your father. Scoot."

Later she said, "He was so young."

And our father: "He let a stupid thing get the best of him."

"Hansi."

"Ever since he had to wear that hearing aid it was nothing but stupidity and depression. Foolishness."

"It was an accident."

"Foolishness. And not facing up to things."

"Hansi, the police said a tragic accident."

"Yes, I know what they said, but you could so easy see it

coming. Ridiculous black moods over this little thing, a hearing aid. For a man to let that get the best of him when there's so many good things to live for . . ." Father's opinions on suicide were as categorical as his views on unions and the Italian army, which, he liked to say, was as useless as tits on a boar. "Boys" — he turned to us — "nothing is so bad as that, eh?"

He and Mother looked from Ralph to me, searching, I guess, for signs of black moods in our faces, and they both wagged their heads gravely. What were they looking for? A certain tilt to the chin indicating mental imbalance? The tremble of incompetence? Drooling? The sweat of the incipiently deranged?

I saw no signs of them in myself. I was Dickie, the friendly fat kid, the younger brother who slipped through the snakes and ladders of schoolyards and little league with jokes and gentle cunning and a certain brute presence on the football field. Maybe I was a little excessive in my eating habits and in my love of words, but what was that, after all? When I stood before the mirror I saw calm brown eyes looking back at me, uncertainty, and a flicker of not unattractive shiftiness. Also a mole on my right cheek. But none of the lip-biting intensity I saw in my brother Ralph. Nerves, agitation. (Or did I see that later, oh memory eager to take credit?)

Because at first they were not mood swings exactly, what I saw in Ralph. Moments of passion, yes. Joy over kissing Margo Bunkowski with the large breasts. "Dickie, Dickie," he confided, sitting on my bed after a date, "I got this close with Margo." He held up his finger and thumb, a tiny space between. He embroidered the story for his lusting younger brother — thighs, panties, mammos.

That was the up side.

The down came when he couldn't get a problem in Badger Mendez's Head Buster book. So ecstasy, yes, but also rage. The stuff of every adolescent's pathetic drama — along with pimples, cruising, lover's nuts. But the signs of madness?

If there was anything you noticed about Ralph it was the way he lived in a world where he made the rules. I loved his moods. On the school grounds after his weekly math test he ripped up sheets of foolscap and threw the pieces high above his head. Confetti. Then he leapt about and grabbed your hands, making you cavort with him, twirling about the yard in a wild and reckless dance. He led us in singing obscene parodies of "The Queen," he organized the piss-on-Prungle's-whitewalls contest. Yes, he pulled us along with him on his absorbed and furious dance, a magnet of a creature in my iron-stained youth. He laughed, he howled, he was constantly on the move. You couldn't help but love my brother Ralph.

Or hate him.

At home he stuck his tongue out at Mother while she was talking intently to Father about household furnishings, and when she turned her withering glare on him he smirked his Cheshire cat smile, all teeth and phoniness. He dropped his eyes to his plate, feigning repentance he didn't feel. She returned to her mashed potatoes and the virtues of deep-pile carpeting, and when she was well into the swing of it, he yawned loudly and looked around in mock surprise, as if the yawn had startled him, too. And Mother looked as if she would either break down and cry or slap him in the face. He could be cruel, yes. Cruel as well as captivating.

Here's what I mean. One day I came home from school and spotted him waving from the roof of the house. He began shouting when I was still two houses away. "Look," he cried when I got closer, and he flapped the TV antenna cable in the air above his head. "We're through with that one channel shit. Tui kaka." He jigged on the roof and explained to me breathlessly how he'd broken Red Rock's static grid and tapped into two channels from Minneapolis. In iron-ringed Red Rock, TV reception meant one snowy channel, CBC.

"It's a cinch," he called down when I got to the foot of the ladder propped against the house. "Just invert the magnetic field and zammo. Come up on the roof, Dickie, and see! I just adapted the theory of magnetic poles." (At least I think that's what he said, it was always a mystery to me when he talked physics.) He was so eager for me to witness his triumph

21

he danced right to the roof's edge with the antenna cable. "Come on, Dickie, come on." I held my breath as he teetered on the eavestrough, shoetops beetling over, heedless of the twelve-foot drop. But he did not fall. Not then.

From below, his hands looked small and delicate, a girl's hands. The shock of straw hair stuck up on the crown of his head like an explosion. He tilted above me, oblivious to the dangers of falling, and I held my breath, I seem to recall. He was grinning and feeling swell about himself, while I sweated below and wanted to shout what Mother would have: *Ralphie, be careful!*

And the next day, it seemed, I came into his room and found him with his head clutched in his hands, a parody of despair, only it was real. He was moaning and rocking sideways to some tune only he could hear. Torn papers littered the floor. A textbook lay face down with the pages crumpled.

"Dickie, Dickie," he moaned, "I'll never make it."

He was referring to the advanced physics he was studying by correspondence from the University of Toronto.

"You will. Mr. Rook will help you."

"Nuts to that, Dickie. Old Rook wouldn't know an isotope if one came up to him in the street and bit him in the butt."

"Or Dr. Mendez."

"Badger Mendez! He knows even less than Rook — "

That was the first time I realized how alone he was. For the most part he'd educated himself, the student turned master, sweating out proofs in his room with only sheaves of mimeoed solutions to tell him if he'd got the concepts. A heavy load for teenage shoulders inclined to the basketball court, to dates in Chevrolets, to "Dragnet." And for emotional support a befuddled kid brother absorbed by Bazooka gum and baseball cards with only the habitual shrug of the good loser to offer in moments of crisis.

And the next day, it seemed, the next day his room was chaos complete: papers heaped on the floor, bedclothes scattered about, spilled ink, broken pottery, books strewn everywhere. A sweet odor filled the air. Ralph lay on the bed, shoes off, toes waggling. His toenails were long and dirty. He had his ankles crossed. He nursed a tumbler of Hansi's whiskey in his hands.

"It's all over," he announced. "Fini."

He meant the exam on organic chemistry, which had come in a sealed envelope from the University of Toronto.

"Bad?" I asked.

"Screwed entirely. Effing-tirely." That was another thing about Ralph. He loved swearing.

"How do you know?"

"Dickie, don't be a pinhead."

"But Mr. Ligham says — "

He threw a book at me. It sailed past my head into the hall. "Shit. Even you know more than Liver-face Ligham. That boob."

I was willing to bet against it, but there was nothing you could say. Arguing just made him violent. I gave the usual shrug.

"A trucker. That's what you're looking at now, Dickie my boy. The open road. La nefermita vojo. Miles of nothing but more miles and miles: no problems, no tests, no California Institute of effing Technology. Just me and the open highway. Country and Western music, you see, and Pabst beer at roadside joints called Mercury Bar and Old West Saloon. And, yes, let's not forget Peggy-Sue bringing lemon pie and hot coffee. Varmega kafo." His lips trembled. He swigged Hansi's rye. It dribbled down his chin and spotted the front of his T-shirt amber, like the iron stains dotting everything in Red Rock.

"It might not be so bad."

"What insight, younger brother," he sneered, "what linebacker genius."

Yes, he could be cruel, it was the flip side of his manic glee.

He added, "Of course, I forget the travel. I might even get to California." He paused and then whispered to himself, "In a pig's eye, I will."

I saw then the stack of *Playboys* at his elbow and recalled

Ralph confiding to me that he and Matt Stockton had hired a hooker at the Rockland Hotel for prom night. He said he'd do the same for me one day, though just the thought of talking to a girl made my palms sweat. Ralph noticed I'd spotted the *Playboy*s and threw them aside with a loud groan.

He took every setback hard, but this was the worst I'd seen. And he didn't even know for sure it was a setback. He'd only just posted the sealed envelope. If it was me I would have laughed it off. Anyone else would at least have waited for the results before raving and cursing. But not Ralph, not the wunderkind. With him it was all good or all bad, all up or all down. Violent. Mood swings. It was all he knew.

Five

Hansi Frudel knew one thing: he loved his wife. He loved her more than his business, more than himself, more than his sons. *Love* was not a word a man like Hansi used much. He would not have used it, for one thing, to describe the bond that grows among men who fight and die together, though that was a kind of caring he had learned in Italy, a kind of loving. He might sometimes have thought the affection he felt for his sons, an affection that meant he would automatically lay down his life for them, was love. He might have said that. What he felt for Tina was neither of these. For her he cared passionately and completely.

Why? It wasn't her beauty, though she was attractive in an unconventional way — big-boned with a strong jaw and crystal blue eyes. She wasn't a particularly brilliant woman, either, or a stunning conversationalist. She danced well, was a first-rate cook, and was pleasant company — all conventional virtues shared by thousands of women of her day. What made Tina preferable to these was a simple trait: she believed in Hansi.

She had come into his life when things were looking bad for him. The Depression was in full swing — block-long lines of men at the casual labor exchange, crowds at the soup kitchens, gangs of unemployed riding boxcars from Vancouver to Montreal and then back again. Hansi had enrolled in business college, but by the spring of 1936 he was working in a coal yard shifting bags of coke and shoveling loose coal from railcar to bin to delivery truck. He worked seven to five, Monday to Saturday, for six bucks a week: soot, dirt, backache. When Hansi looked up from his shoveling in the spring

25

of 1936 he saw before him a life of unending tedium and exhaustion.

This is why Tina was important. Though she too came from a working-class background — her father toiled all his life in the CN rail yards — she shared Hansi's ambitions and believed in his ability to realize them. They were modest enough as ambitions go, petty bourgeois, actually: to be independent, to work for himself on his own terms, to own a small business. Yet in 1936 they seemed to Hansi as he shoveled coal for a dollar a day as remote as an office job at Portage and Main.

But Tina kept his spirits up. When his moods were as black as the coal grime permeating his skin, she told him things will work out, things will get better soon and when they do, you will succeed. You're a good man and a hard worker.

So she sustained him through the bad years when Hansi had all but lost faith in himself, and when the war came she supported his wish to enlist, too, even though she had a baby and might have insisted, as other wives did, he stay home with her. Instead she said, "Go," and he had gone. And when he returned she was waiting at the railway station, one boy clinging to her skirts, her felt hat with the peacock feather perched on her head, and the other on her hip.

Hansi came back with a Distinguished Service Cross on his chest, a reaction to heat that brought on mysterious rashes and boils, and a heart full of sad memories. These were mental tableaux, actually. A colonel shot by his own men was one; another the bloodied stump of a gunner's arm landing at his feet, still another the terror on an Italian peasant's face as Hansi turned a flame-thrower on him — it was a reflex, the peasant had a grenade, but still. These were things he could never repeat to Tina, but things that made him a more caring and gentle man, a better husband than he might otherwise have been.

And he was a good husband. The miners of Red Rock noticed it. They were a foul-mouthed lot, loud beer drinkers who caroused and fought over women and fell face down drunk in the street. Two-Bottle Hansi never swore, a fact all the more impressive since he'd been in the heat of battle and seen men at their worst. The women of Red Rock thought he was marvelous, a born gentleman. He stepped aside on the street when a woman passed, he never ran his gaze up and down their bodies. He went shopping at the Safeway with Tina, and in the evenings out for ice cream at the Dairy Queen with the boys. He was a family man.

Yes, Hansi was devoted to Tina. At home he would put down his newspaper, seize her hand and look into her eyes.

"I love you, too, Hansi," she'd respond, surprised at her knitting, and a little perplexed. She stroked the inside of his forearm the way he liked, a prelude to slipping off to the bedroom together.

"Sometimes — "

"Yes, Hansi?"

"It doesn't matter."

He knew if anything ever happened to her he would be desperate. He knew, too, how close that had come to happening.

Though she had a bony build, Tina also had narrow hips, a family trait. Her mother had suffered terribly during childbirth. And when Tina had gone to the hospital to have Ralph, there'd been a horrifying episode. First the baby was overdue many days. Normal, the doctors said, with the first. But when the labor intensified, the child wouldn't come. One hour passed, two. Tina sweated everywhere — forehead, throat, wrists. She soaked her nightshirt through.

Six hours passed, twelve.

Tina bit her lower lip until it bled. Hansi said to the doctors, "Do something. There must be drugs for this pain."

But not when a baby's life was at risk. Brain damage, the doctors warned, mental retardation, God knows what. They shook their heads and exhorted Tina to push harder. She gritted her teeth, blood flowed from her mouth. And then Tina — who had been brave through the first twenty hours — began screaming.

Hansi said to the doctors: "*This* is causing brain damage. And look at my poor wife. Look at her, you quacks!"

27

Later Tina whispered to Hansi, "Give me water." And after drinking, "I have to confess something, Hansi. I've been lying here praying to God to save me. At first I prayed save me and the baby. But then when the pain got so bad I wavered. Save *me*, I begged, only take away this pain. Now I can't pray anymore. I cannot. It hurts so bad I just want it to be over. Just to be over, you understand? Even if I die."

Hansi threatened the doctors. He was a small, wiry man, but he stuck out his jaw in a fierce way. When he got angry he looked as if he might be capable of anything — he might kill if one of his family were suffering. He made this clear.

The doctors sent him to the waiting room while they operated. And twenty minutes later Ralph uttered his first cries. But the questions Hansi asked the doctors were about Tina, and he wept holding her hand as she came out of the anesthetic.

The second time Tina went into labor Hansi was in Europe in 1942. The doctors operated as soon as Tina was admitted. And Hansi wrote to tell her that the scars were nothing to be ashamed of, students in Germany scarred each other's cheeks to show manliness. Tina cried about that — and because she had wanted a girl. But Hansi wrote saying the baby was wonderful, a fat little beauty. *Dick*, he said, is German for fat, and he's our little Dickie.

Still Tina wanted a girl, and though the doctor warned against a third pregnancy, a third operation, she talked Hansi into trying again as soon as he came back from Europe, and she went into labor convinced she would have a beautiful, smart, and strong little girl. It was Hansi who was worried. He feared for his Tina, whom he needed so much, who stood beside him no matter what. Why had he let her talk him into this foolishness?

When the doctor came into the waiting room Hansi knew something dreadful had happened. Complications, the doctor said, fluids threatening ruptures in places Hansi hadn't heard of, much less understood. What he did understand was this: if they took the chance delivering the baby they might lose it or Tina — or both. The consequences were horrible, but

28

Hansi didn't hesitate a moment. He didn't take the time to pray. The choice had been made by Tina a decade before when she stood beside him.

And so Hansi sent Tina's baby to her grave. Her little black-haired girl. He did it because nothing was more important than Tina. But what a decision. At the store sometimes Hansi caught himself staring into space and he knew some inadvertent sound had made him recall his lost baby. Perhaps the squeak of a carriage passing the door of Hansi's Hardware, or the distant cooing of a mother. He'd never told Tina what the doctors told him, what he'd decided on his own and in agony, because it was better she think the baby had died of natural causes. It was a horrible thing to do, send an unborn child to the grave, but Hansi knew he would do the same thing again. There was nothing, there was no one, as important as Tina.

Six

On Fridays after school and all day Saturday I worked at Hansi's Hardware. While my classmates kibitzed on street corners, smoked cigarettes, whistled at the girls from the Catholic school, drank Cokes at Len Ho's Café, I prepared to enter the real world according to Hansi Frudel: Commerce, Prudence, and Industry. First he gave me a canvas apron, compliments of Benjamin Moore Paints, and a stubby pencil to poke behind my ear. Then he gave me instructions. My primary tasks were in the stock room. I unloaded paint cans from their crates, sorted them according to brand, type, and color, stacked them on the shelves, labels facing out. For the first quarter hour he worked beside me, encouraging, correcting, making sure the job was done right.

There was a warm glow about him then. He puffed as he worked, cheeks flushed, and when he stopped he pulled a red polka-dot handkerchief from his pocket and daubed his brow. Did I say he'd picked up a bug of some kind in Italy and was susceptible to heat? His skin burst into boils when he perspired a lot. But he loved simple tasks — like stacking bags of peat moss onto wooden pallets, or arranging paint cans on shelves, or sweeping the cement floor with a push broom after sprinkling it with damp sawdust. He would stand in a room after sweeping with Lysol and savor the air. For my father simple tasks were as satisfying as games of chance or chasing women were to other men.

He expected me to work beside him as an equal, each with a job to do, each pulling his own weight. He made a game of it, challenging me to keep up, and when we were going along nicely he'd put his hand on my elbow and whisper, "That's the way, son." His gentle touch was electric. That was greater encouragement than praise from the football coach, or teachers at school. It was casual, offered almost unnoticed in an hour of routine, but from my father who laughed at Hopeless Mike's ineptitudes, it was praise you hungered to hear. And then, "That's it, you've got it now, son."

So I worked. Always carefully. Always trying to get as much accomplished as possible without making errors of haste. How I stacked those cans in perfect rows, labels facing out, dusted to a bright shine. To please my father. He was not a taskmaster but a quiet man who owned a small business and ran it by the sweat of his brow. Who worked hard and never complained. There was a quiet dignity about him. He was a war hero who'd fought Nazis and fascists in Europe and came back with medals and yet never bragged about his exploits, who put in a full day's work and expected the same from any man. I hung on his words. I wanted to please him. So I sweated out his every instruction. Shifted and stacked and carried and swept while the crowd at Len Ho's, Ralph included, flirted and joked and sucked back Cokes and frittered away Saturday afternoons in the trivial sun.

When I stopped to admire my work, I sometimes squared my shoulders, fantasizing I was a linebacker for the Winnipeg Blue Bombers. Or I fancied myself a returning war hero. I wanted to be like my father more than anyone else in the world. Even more than I wanted to be like my brother Ralph, who was by all accounts, not just those of a brother grateful for extra TV channels and help with desperate homework, a genius. Ralph, who delighted us with his manic flights, his zany defiance of authority — in an era of authority: Containment, Agonizing Re-appraisal, the Berlin Wall.

My God, the antics.

He brought his physics homework to school one day on a folded piece of six-by-eight cardboard, and presented it to Mr. Rook with a bow and a flourish as the work of an artist. He glued the pages of Badger Mendez's favorite text together with horse dung. He broke up the assembly with

31

his impersonation of Liver-face Ligham's cockney accent. Ralph, who did not have to stack and sweep on Friday nights and all day Saturday.

When exactly an hour and a half had passed, Father would appear in the doorway with two Pepsi-Colas. It was time for our break. He'd hand me one bottle and we'd sit on the wooden bench in back while we rested. He'd gawk around. "You're doing a good job."

"Thanks," I said glumly, thinking of Ralph.

Reading my mind he said, "Be grateful you're not so smart like your brother." I didn't reply, but he knew I was thinking of how Ralph didn't have to work at the store. He came right to the point. "It isn't so bad working here, is it? And I pay you." That was true. He paid me the same wage as Hopeless Mike, the other side of having to work beside him as an equal.

I muttered, "I like it," only half lying.

"So you see. And your brother Ralph, what will he be doing tomorrow when you and me are listening to the Braves on the radio? Out on the town having a good time? Cruising Main Street with his school chums?" We both knew the answer. Studying.

"Studying. That kind of fun I would rather be without, Dickie, if you ask me. Personally." He left a silence for both of us to think, a silence in which he sipped from his bottle of Pepsi and I watched his Adam's apple bob as he swallowed. "Can all that studying be good for a person?"

"I have dreams, too."

"Ah, dreams. I am not such a pinhead, as you kids say, not to see that. But dreams are best to keep them simple. Simple."

Hopeless Mike came into the room looking for an invoice book, and after Father had told him they were on a shelf under the front counter, stood absently in the doorway waiting to be dismissed. So Father dismissed him.

"Not simple like this, mind you," whispered Father, nodding in Mike's direction and smiling conspiratorially. "But us ordinary joes, Dickie, we're better off like we are than in the shoes of your brother Ralph."

He waited for me to ask why, and when I did not, continued. "Complicated, I mean so complicated it's not healthy. Fidgety, anxious. Your uncle Emmanuel was like this. And countless men in the army. Guys with too much on their minds to enjoy the simple things life has to offer. Like drinking Pepsi." He smiled and sipped at his. "Guys who have to have the best — the best house, the best car, the best job — each guy with a different best but all the same in the end. Because to get the best you have to chase. And chasing is the root of unhappiness. You smile, eh, thinking it should be the other way around? But chasing, Dickie, is the root of all evil."

That was easy to say when Ralph was at Len Ho's playing the jukebox and I was expected to learn about the real world with a stubby pencil and a push broom. Father produced his red hankie and wiped his brow before adding, "Chasing. In the end, unhappiness comes from chasing — money, women — from not being content with what you have. And happiness is what counts."

Yes, I thought, but who is really happy, Hansi Frudel with his hardware store in a two-bit mining town looking at no future except passing the business on to his failed younger son — along with the hi-fi and the rusty Meteor — or Ralph Bascom Frudel, boy genius destined for the golden life in California? It was obvious to me, but I knew there was a low-down cunning to my father I had to take into account. He'd been right about the Braves going to the World Series. He could be right about this, too.

Sometimes when I saw my brother Ralph pulling his hair over a problem in math or physics I thought Father was right. Ralph seemed touchy about petty things, about the arrangement of pencils on his desk, about noises in the house while he was studying, things I began to see as obsessions. I watched the way he dug at his ear with the blunt end of a pencil and wondered why he always folded his dirty underwear before putting it in the laundry basket. Were these signs of something? He was so up when things went good that it took me a while to see the same crazed intensity in his happiness as in his sadness. There was something not quite real about it.

I thought about my desire to go to Toronto and wondered if that was unreal, too. Mrs. Prungle's photos had sparked a powerful desire in me, an urge I could not express even to myself but had something to do with crowds and stone buildings and the scent of women's perfume. It was not the desire to do something big in the world, which I saw in Ralph and other brainy students, or the desire to control money, things, and people, which flushed the faces of the ambitious. I couldn't put a name to it but it set my toes tapping when I sat at my desk at school, it sent words rushing to my mouth in torrents. It was the reason I was not performing brilliantly in class or living up to my famous potential — famous in my report cards only. It was the dreamy look I was accused of having. But most of all it was the restless urge behind my sweeping, my stacking, my puffing at Hansi's Hardware on Friday nights and every Saturday afternoon.

Seven

Though she had been to visit the family after the death of Ann-Marie, Tina's sister, Ellen, had not been in Red Rock for ten years. She had spent most of her visit in 1947 admonishing Tina not to cry over the lost baby, and perhaps the prospect of going through that again had been too painful. So the family was surprised to hear she was coming to Red Rock that fall of 1957.

Ellen lived in a ritzy part of Toronto with her dentist husband, Albert, whom she couldn't stop bragging about whenever she telephoned Red Rock. Albert this, Albert that. Catalogues of new and expensive purchases, emphasizing how well they were doing: a powerboat, broadloom, vacations in Hawaii. All in a high nasal twang that pierced the ears.

Hansi said, "That voice would drive me to the grave."

No matter what she had installed in the house, it suited her for no longer than it took the dust to settle. One month after installation, the automatic washer and dryer had to be shifted from the basement to the second story and the second story remodeled to accommodate them.

"Always changing her mind," Hansi said when he heard about this. "Up and down more often than a toilet seat at a mixed party."

Her voice was brassy. Tina heard her complaining before she was off the train at the Red Rock station. "Careful with those leather cases!" she screeched at the porter. "They're not wooden crates." And when she spotted Tina, "Look what this oaf's done to the calfskin bags I bought in Florence. The idea. He should be made to pay for them. He should be fired." She wagged one finger, the rings on the others flashing. "If my Albert was here . . ."

The sisters embraced. They looked each other over. Tina said, lying in the way of sisters, "You're looking good."

"And so are you," Ellen answered brightly, since that was the thing to say, even though both of them knew it wasn't true. Tina was wearing a yellow dress, its sunny color was supposed to lift her spirits. They stood in strained silence for a few moments and then embraced again to relieve the tension before Tina picked up one of Ellen's bags and directed her to the car.

In Ellen's presence Tina felt overshadowed. Ellen was three years older than her. When they had lived at home with their mother, Tina had done the housework while Ellen and her mother listened to soap operas on the radio and drank coffee. Her mother developed fainting spells when she stood over the kitchen sink, she said, and Ellen did such a terrible job of vacuuming that even when she condescended to it, Tina had to do the job all over again. So Tina lived under Ellen's shadow.

At school it was the same. Ellen was popular where Tina seemed always to say the wrong thing and get called a goody-goody or a pill. When Ellen dated boys Tina had to stay up half the night listening to the details. When she was finished her accounts, Tina was required to fetch Ellen a glass of warm milk for her nerves.

So Tina went to Red Rock's railway station feeling a mixture of expectation and despair. She wanted to unburden her heart about her stomach pains and vomiting. She wanted Ellen to hold her while she purged herself in tears. But she knew Ellen would be not only unaware of her but shrill and demanding.

On the drive home Tina said, "I'm glad you're here."

Ellen gazed out the car window and sobbed, "It's so obvious?"

"You look a little tired. That train ride . . ."

"Don't be a moron."

"It's just fatigue."

"It's not fatigue. I'm — it's cancer."

That was at the height of Tina's obsession with tea. It was years since she'd trashed the percolator and smashed her favorite coffee mug to smithereens with a hammer. Now she had a china teapot and a set of Dresden cups and drank only tea. At first she'd used the standard brands from Safeway: Red Rose Orange Pekoe, Blue Ribbon. Then one day she stumbled across some exotic brands and bought a book and read about boiling the water until it formed bubbles the size of marbles, of steaming the pot, of steeping for three minutes and then removing the bag. She read about infusion and about tea eggs, and she bought one. Then a visiting cousin bragged about the herbal teas in Vancouver. The cousin sent by mail small packets of English Breakfast, Darjeeling, Queen Mary, Irish Breakfast, and Jasmine, and when Tina had sampled these and declared for the Jasmine and Queen Mary, the cousin sent Earl Grey, Chamomile, Caravan, Apricot, Rosehip, Gunpowder, Ginger, and Mint. Tina tried them all. Her favorite was Gunpowder, she loved the way the leaves expanded, exploded almost in the water.

Over the years she became a connoisseur, interrupting gossip sessions to comment on water purity and Safeway's shameful practice of dumping tailings into tea bags. She waxed poetic over the scent of Mint and the body of Earl Grey until one day Hansi made a joke about Tina's love of Earl Grey's body. Like all connoisseurs she became a bore.

But she made a fine pot of tea. In the kitchen Ellen dried her tears and sipped a fresh cup of Earl Grey. Tina asked, "So how long have you known?" Her voice trembled. She'd had a premonition about fatal disease ever since she'd started feeling pains in the side and vomiting in the mornings.

"The first tests were March, but my doctor clammed up until the specialists had their go at me too. Tests and more tests. Poke here, sample that. It seems like years."

In the bright light of the kitchen Tina noted the dark hollows under Ellen's eyes and her sister's sallow skin and she shuddered, thinking these were the tell-tale signs of wasting. Ellen looked weak and distracted.

"And — ?"

Ellen stared into her cup. "It's leukemia, they say. Blood cancer. Of course they hold out hope. New drugs, they say, are being tested every day, and some doctor in Rochester is working on a machine. There's cobalt, there's radium treatments which make your hair fall out. There's blood transfusions, endless needles. You wouldn't believe the holes I've got in my arms, Tina. You'd think I was a heroin addict." She lifted one arm, intending to reveal the blue pinpricks on her skin, and then thinking better, returned it to the table.

"I wouldn't like that."

"Pain is unbecoming, Tina. But death — "

"Don't say that. It's a sign of despair."

"I'm only thinking of the radium treatments. Last week I got to watch how they do it. The doctors thought it best. Familiarize myself. Tina, the way those women look. They've all lost their hair. One of them sat beside me on the bench and cried for an hour before they took her in, and do you know when she got up from the bench there were rings of sweat on the leather she was so scared. Sweat rings the size of plates." Ellen held up her hands and made a plate shape in the air.

"This was just last week?"

"The funny thing is I never thought anything like this could happen to me. Mother used to say I was the tough dame in the family. I hated her for that. But I never missed a day at school. Not one."

"You got a certificate for that."

"Not one."

"You were always so healthy."

"Remember my project on dental hygiene?"

"First prize in the science fair. Mother was so proud."

"And now — " Ellen poured another cup of tea.

"Maybe . . ."

"It isn't fair, Tina, it just isn't fair. You think, why can't it be someone else who gets the bad luck."

"I know. I know."

"Why can't it be someone else who dies." Ellen put her

hand over her mouth as if she'd sworn in church. "What an idiot," she whispered.

"You're upset."

"That was a stupid thing to say."

"It doesn't matter."

"You may not believe this after what you've been through, Tina, but life is precious. It's all there is. And it's the only thing that matters."

Tina had been thinking the same thing. And more, too. Wasn't leukemia hereditary? She recalled two brothers in Red Rock had died of it within a year. It was leukemia, she was certain. Blood disease in any case. Yes, it was the Kropo bachelors who lived in a tar-paper shack on the edge of town, and they died within months of each other barely a year after the first one found out there was something wrong. And she was sure it had been leukemia. But in her heart she was praying it wasn't and if it was, this time, this time God don't let it be me.

Eight

Father liked to loosen his tie, roll up the sleeves of his white shirt, and enjoy the role of proprietor. Sometimes when Hopeless Mike and I were working in back he stood on the sidewalk out front of the store surveying Red Rock's main street. The Safeway was being repainted. The Red Rock Theater's marquee announced "Rebel Without a Cause" would show twice on both Friday and Saturday through the month. A new Shell service station stood kitty-corner to Hansi's. It was the newest building in town and it was two years old. Development in Red Rock had ground to a standstill. Sure, there was the Union Hall two blocks down, erected the summer previous, and the town council had finally built a new fire station. This was merely window dressing in Father's opinion.

Father worried about this. He'd heard a famous million-aire on TV say a business standing still was actually going backward. And mining towns had a way of flaring up and dying down. Remember Elliot Lake, he'd ask me, where the richest gold mines in the country gave out when things were looking good? In no time flat nothing but a ghost town: empty storefronts, echoing streets, defeated dreams, houses lost on mortgages.

The miners clumping into Hansi's Hardware in their iron-stained boots brought news with them, gossip actually, about fights between foremen and laborers, about women, about sex scandals. In Red Rock someone was always sleeping with someone else's wife, one miner punching out an-other behind the Rockland Hotel. Quarrels at dances, knife fights, gang bangs, beatings: the life of a mining town. Every year at least one bloody murder, the flashpoint of some sexual powderkeg, had everyone in town whispering and shaking heads for months. Miners loved to talk about these things, and though Father listened to their gossip, he glanced worriedly over his shoulder from time to time, thinking their talk was not something I should be hearing. He nodded, he laughed at appropriate places. He had an ulterior motive.

What concerned Father were the goings-on in the mining company boardrooms. So he chatted up the men who came into his store, especially those who worked in the offices and who picked up news about what the mine executives were thinking and what the union's big bosses in New York and Chicago were up to. This was information crucial to a businessman — especially one who worried about the town's future, as Father did.

Gerry Stockton came in every week. He was a beefy man in his mid-thirties, already running to fat from his desk job at the mine. He worked in an office on the accounts. His son, Matt, was in the same grade at school as Ralph. For a big man Gerry was high-strung. When the talk turned to sex he drummed his fingers on the counter; when it turned to mine politics he chain-smoked.

He asked, "What's the big panic around here today?" Hopeless Mike was unpacking cases of rifle shells and stacking boxes on shelves as fast as he was able.

"That special moose season," Father answered, "opened at midnight."

"That explains why the highway to the mine was so plugged this morning. You'd think it was the Irish rebellion."

Father chuckled. "As good as." He dropped his voice to a whisper. He had taken out his pocketknife and was nicking gold hairs off his forearm with its razor-sharp edge. "With all those drunken idiots out there popping off at the first thing to move, a man runs a greater risk of being shot than he did in Italy."

Gerry laughed. "Right. I felt safer at Rapallo." Gerry and Father laughed together, and I stuck my head out of the stock room when I heard their cackling.

41

Hopeless Mike, carrying an armload of cartons, interrupted Father to ask where the empty boxes from the shotgun shells went. Father pointed to the back of the store. When Mike disappeared into the recesses of the stock room he whispered, "I don't know how that Mike can be messing up so much in a job."

"At least he has one."

"Eh?"

Gerry took a pack of cigarettes out of his breast pocket and lighted one, eyes fixed on Father. He flicked the smoldering match to the floor. "Rumor has it the company's thinking of bringing in conveyor belts."

"And replacing how many men? A hundred? Two?"

"Rumor also has it the men are going out on wildcat."

"Like I told you last week," said Father. His dislike of unions went back a long way. It began in the thirties when he'd worked in a meat-packing plant to put himself through business college. (A story we'd heard round the dinner table it seemed a hundred times.) In the struggle to unionize, Father had been on the losing side and it cost him his job. He'd held it against all unions. A lot of layabouts, he maintained. "All unions ever do is build up the working joe's expectations and leave him out in the cold when the crunch comes," he argued. "All the union ever protects is the union — and its bosses." Such opinions were not popular in Red Rock. Whenever Father started talking this way around the store I got a knot in my stomach. I imagined those opinions coming back to haunt me on the schoolyard.

With Gerry, Father had a more sympathetic audience than with most miners. "What are they after," he asked, "with this wildcat?"

"They claim it's to keep the conveyor belts out." Gerry watched smoke rings curl to the ceiling. "But if you ask me, it's money, plain and simple," he said.

"Money," Father snorted.

Before Gerry could answer a third voice said, "Dead right." It was Bill Russell's, a miner who worked underground and played on the town's senior hockey team. A tough. His son Shreve was in my class at school. Bill Russell had come in when Father had his back turned at the counter, and he was standing at the rear of the store looking at hunting rifles.

Father glanced at Gerry and bit his lower lip. "But you make the best wages in the country already. In the world, maybe," he said, throwing his voice to the back of the store. Then he said, "All the more power to you, as far as I'm concerned, but antagonizing the company only leads to one thing. You know that, Bill."

"I do, do I," Bill Russell said. He put his hands on his hips and walked toward Father. His black boots clumped on the tiles. "You tell me anyway, Hansi."

Father's lips were set. He knew he should back down, but instead he said, "It leads to the whole town going dead. While you guys are out on strike trying to settle with the mine, we all sit around idle. It could be two, three months." Father had stopped nicking the hairs off his arm and he folded his pocket knife up carefully and put it in his pocket.

"So?"

"Seems to me you're further behind than if you'd never gone out." Father's voice wavered when he said this, but he stuck his chin out as Bill Russell came up the aisle toward him.

Bill Russell placed one hand on the counter. From behind, his back looked big and solid. "And what business is it of yours? That's what I'd like to know."

"Just that," Father said. "Business." He looked at Gerry, who was lighting one cigarette off another, dropping the butt to the floor and grinding it out with his toe. "I've got a family to feed and mortgages to pay, just like you do, Bill, but I don't have a union to look out for me. Bunch of guys with slicked-back hair and a morality to match who live in Chicago and pull the strings of their puppets in Red Rock."

"If you ask me," Bill Russell said, "you should keep that Kraut nose of yours out of things that don't concern you."

I'd been standing in the stock room doorway, listening. Hopeless Mike had come up behind me. I could feel his hot breath on my neck. He placed one hand on my shoulder.

43

Father wiped his hands on his apron. He stepped quickly from behind the counter. "That sounds like a threat to me."

"Yeah?"

"Hey, hey," said Gerry Stockton. He stepped forward, as if meaning to come between Father and Bill Russell, but Father raised one forearm and blocked him back.

"Yeah," Father said to Bill Russell. "And I don't take threats from anyone. Not anywhere or any time but especially not on my own property."

Bill Russell snorted. He was a head taller than Father and he stepped toward him, lunged actually, and pushed him with one hand in the center of the chest. He was wearing a big gold wristwatch and it glittered on the end of his arm. I guess he expected Father to collapse or something because when he didn't Bill Russell looked surprised.

That's when Father punched him, not hard, but sharply, right in the Adam's apple. He grunted doing it and then Bill Russell crumpled to the floor, making gagging sounds as he fell, trying to catch his breath. His arms flopped crazily at his sides.

We all just stood there for a moment, Father pushing at the sleeves of his white shirt, Gerry Stockton with a cigarette in his lips, Hopeless Mike with his hand still on my shoulder. Father's voice seemed to come from far away. "I don't like threats." He said this to Gerry. "See. I don't like people coming onto my property making threats."

Gerry knelt beside Bill Russell. He'd dropped his cigarette and smoke curled up from it. He was saying, "Jesus, Hansi."

Hopeless Mike stepped around me. "My God," he said. "My God."

"Call someone," Gerry said. He nodded toward the phone.

Hopeless Mike stood at the counter running his hands up and down his thighs. "My God," he repeated.

"The police," Gerry said. "Call an ambulance." He was looking at Bill Russell's legs, which were twitching, clocking the heels of his black boots on the floor.

"It's all right," Father said. His chest was heaving and his breath coming in short gasps, as mine was, but his voice was steady. "He'll be all right. I didn't kill him."

I was relieved to hear that because I'd heard Father say he'd learned in the army how to kill a man with one punch to the throat and I thought I'd just seen it happen.

I walked into the room and looked at Bill Russell lying on the floor. His eyes had rolled up in their sockets. He was getting his breath back but his face was purple. He coughed and choked like a swimmer who'd swallowed a mouthful of water. It was clear he wasn't going to die.

I sighed then, and Father put his big hand on my shoulder. His touch was light but his skin was hot. "Not on my property," he whispered to me. "You understand that, don't you?"

Nine

No one in Red Rock was immune to rumors. In history class Mr. Beyers said, "A wildcat is an illegal strike." It was snot-nosed Lester Sheldon who asked and he made a doodle in his notebook right under Beyers's nose while the teacher answered.

"No sirree bob," Shreve Russell said from the back. His voice had the same irritating bluntness as his father's.

Patsy Johnson swiveled to smile at Shreve and then turned back to Mr. Beyers. "What Shrevey means is the miners have rights, too. Like we learned in civics class about."

"What I mean," said Shreve, raising his voice and driving a nail into it, "is that strikes ain't illegal no more."

"Aren't," said Mr. Beyers. "Aren't illegal, any longer." While the class was tittering, he perched on Margo Bunkowski's desk at the best angle to peek down the front of her dress. When the class was silent again he continued. "But Shrevey's right about strikes. At least so far as they're organized and called by the elected officers of the union. That's a legal strike and it has the company's and the union's sanction, too. But when the men walk off the job on their own, over the heads of their elected leaders, so to speak, that's an illegal strike. A wildcat strike."

"A revolution, sort of," I said, and felt my ears turning red as my voice echoed round the classroom. Did I say I have big ears that stick out the side of my head like handles on water jugs? Legacy of my grandfather who shopped at Safeway barefoot and also had abnormal ears.

"Exactly, Frudel," Mr. Beyers said. "When the mass of men seizes power from its leaders we have revolution. We studied that last term when we looked at France. Remember the Tennis Court Oath? And last week when this question first came up I said that unions were an agent of what? Sheldon?"

"Of Ned Morgan," Shreve said, glaring across at Lawrence Morgan, whose father was the local union rep, and hoping Lawrence would want to settle this later.

Mr. Beyers said dryly, "Very funny."

Patsy turned in her seat again. "Ew," she said. "I don't think you'd like us calling down your father, Shrevey." She smiled, showing her straight white teeth. "Before the whole class."

"Thank you, Patsy." Mr. Beyers took a deep breath. "Now, let's get back to our subject. Because unions are an agent of what?"

"Democracy," I said flatly.

The bell rang and Lester Sheldon just had time to write down "dumbocracy" before he slammed his books shut.

And in the hall Shreve said, "Nobody asked for your two cents' worth, fatty." He'd cornered me against the book lockers. I looked into his pale blue eyes. He was captain of the hockey team and a head taller than anyone else in the class. He had a ducktail and wore his collar up like a hardrock. He loved to fight. I clenched and unclenched my fists. I was on the football team, only the reserve squad, true, but I wasn't about to back down. I pressed my hands against my thighs. "Nuts to you," I muttered.

Shreve grabbed my shoulder. "How's that?"

Lawrence Morgan tugged my arm. "C'mon," he said.

"Hey, Krauthead," said Shrevey, "your girlfriend's calling."

I dodged past him and said under my breath, "Peddle your union bullshit somewheres else, mucus membrane."

"Who says it's bullshit?" Shreve loomed over me suddenly, shoving me backward into an open locker. "Your old man, I bet. With his nickel-and-dime business. His Nazi skunk-and-junk."

"You leave my dad out of this."

"Why, fatso? Something to hide?" Shreve pushed up close and grabbed my collar. "He shoulda been shot over there."

"Oh yeah?" I clenched one fist into a ball.

"C'mon," said Lawrence Morgan. He tried to get between us.

But Shreve dodged around him so his face was right up against mine. "Shot with those other Nazi fairies."

Though I hadn't expected to, I punched him just below the eye. I saw blood spurt from Shreve's nose before feeling his fingers claw my throat, felt my windpipe squashed in his grip. When we fell to the concrete floor, Shreve's fingers shook loose for a moment and I gulped back one gasp of air before my face hit the floor. Nose mashed sideways. The tile was cool on my skin. I lost consciousness momentarily but recovered just before Shreve lifted my head by the hair and smashed it down.

I gasped.

The second time my head struck the floor dozens of lights exploded in my eyes. I heard Lawrence shrieking Shreve's name, his voice the hollow echo at the end of a long culvert. I heard Mr. Beyers's classroom door open. Saw feet scurrying down the hall. Heard voices, heard ringing in my ears. I thought, this bastard's going to kill me, I'll die without feeling a girl's breasts.

Then I heard a dull whack like a hockey stick smacked against frozen boards and felt the grip on my throat relax. Shreve Russell groaned.

Mr. Beyers yelled, "Stop, stop!" A grunt. Mr. Beyers yelled, "Ralph!" Then a second dull whack and Mr. Beyers's voice drained away. More feet scurrying down halls.

And in the principal's office Prungle closed the door behind us with a sharp smack. He stood a foot away from us and breathed heavily. "God," he said to Ralph. "What have you done?" He didn't seem to notice I was in the room. "A member of the Student Council and scholarship candidate to Cal Tech?"

"I'm sorry," Ralph said. We were seated beside each other in green leather chairs.

Prungle prowled the room. "You strike a boy with a baseball bat and all you can say is you're sorry?"

"He was killing my goddamn brother."

"He was knocked unconscious. You know how scared we are something serious has happened? And Mr. Beyers!" Prungle rifled through papers on his desk, seized a file folder as if meaning to read it, and then changed his mind. "What will Dr. von Braun say? NASA?"

"NASA cares about liquid fuels and platinum alloys, not moronic Shrevey Russell. Or what happens in the halls of Red Rock bloody High. They could give a tinker's damn about — "

"Don't you dare swear in this office. You haven't got so far above us yet, my boy, that you can brawl and swear whenever you please. I am just a little fed up with your attitude."

A bell rang and our heads turned to the clock. Above it hung a plaque with the school's motto: Education Is the Key To Success. Prungle threw the blue file onto his desk, dramatizing exasperation. He took a short breath and looked out the window. Iron-stained cars crawled along the iron-stained street to the mines. The site that had been cleared for the Baptist Church the summer before and then abandoned when the layoffs began stared back blankly.

The phone on Prungle's desk rang sharply. He snatched it up. "All right," he sighed into the receiver, "that's good. Yes, he's with me now." When he hung up he sighed again. "You had the faculty's unanimous election. Do you know how hard Dr. Mendez worked for that? So RRH could give you a scholarship to the most famous college in the entire United States of America? And now . . ."

"It was my fault," I blurted out.

"You." Prungle fixed me with a stare. "I don't want to hear another word from you." He turned his attention back to Ralph. "Do you know what's involved for us? Dr. von Braun promised new labs and — "

"For you?"

"Yes. What this meant to this school?"

"Meant? Like in the past tense?"

"Yes, past. Can you imagine how word of this will spread

round the town? How it will sound at the Women's Auxiliary and the Rockland Hotel? Shreve's father may press charges. Mr. Beyers may press charges. At the very least the police have to be called in."

"Forget it." Ralph stood.

"What?"

"Forget it. I don't need Dr. Mendez and I don't need you and I don't need your scholarship. Your drippy scholarship."

"You think not?"

"You heard me."

Prungle said, "Wait here." He opened a side door and began barking at his secretary before he was out of the room. I looked at Ralph and then at my feet. I wanted to say something but I didn't know what.

Ralph whispered, "It's okay." He was standing at Prungle's desk, examining the pens and pencils in a ceramic mug while I tried to figure out what I wanted to tell him.

"If he hadn't said that about Dad. About Nazis."

"Hey," Ralph said. "Forget it. They don't get the Frudels down that easy. No dice." With a wink he pocketed a gold pen.

When Prungle returned he said, "Now, young man, we'll see who needs what." He flipped through a file, reading quickly. "Yes. Right here." He held the papers up in front of him. "Your father writes, 'The honor of having our son selected,' blah blah blah. And, yes, here it is, 'In our present circumstances and the future so uncertain we couldn't afford' . . . And so on."

"He'd find a way."

"Don't kid yourself. Your father's a businessman. Financially he's in tough right now. At least he has no illusions."

"You want gratitude? You want us on our knees to you?"

"I want you to realize that having brains doesn't entitle you to spit in the faces of those who have put themselves out on your account. Your parents who worked hard to raise you a God-fearing Christian and respectable citizen, your teachers who give unstintingly of their time and talents, yes, and even paper shufflers like me who have smoothed your way into the most enviable future of any graduate of Red Rock High. You are not entitled."

"Spare me the lecture."

"That's just the point. *Me*. Because you have not only Ralph Bascom Frudel to think about when you take it into your stupid head to scrap in the halls like an animal, going against everything we've tried to teach you here. You have all of us to think of. Your parents, yourself, Red Rock High." He paused for a moment to catch his breath and waved his arm in an arc around the room. "You have the name of the school to consider."

"You want me to crawl on my knees to you?" Ralph stepped suddenly toward Prungle and poked his index finger into the man's chest. "Well, I won't. A Frudel doesn't kiss anybody's ass."

Ten

We walked home from school slowly, intending to stop at Matt Stockton's house to drink Cokes and plan what to tell our parents. "You're really in for it this time," Matt said to Ralph as we climbed the hill into town. "Your old man's gonna have a bird." Like most of our neighbors he'd heard Father shouting at us in the back yard. Hansi was the boss in his house and he didn't mind letting everyone in hearing distance know it. Did I say he'd made the rank of sergeant in the army, that he was used to giving orders and having them obeyed?

"Hey," Matt added suddenly, "the kid's gonna keel over."

It was true. I was putting up a brave front but my legs were wobbly. Every few steps my left knee gave way. We were climbing slowly, Ralph stopping from time to time, waiting for me to catch up. The hilltop looked down on the business section of Red Rock where the big Hansi's Hardware sign peeked past the roof of the Toronto-Dominion Bank. Beyond both, the Pickerel River snaked out of town. In winter it froze over and in summer we fished there, casting spinners and plugs into the sparkling water through the long sunny afternoons. I wished we were fishing in some quiet nook now rather than trudging home to face Father's flushed face and his leather strap, "The Persuader," rarely used but often invoked. Ralph said, "C'mon, Dickie." He put his arm round my shoulder. Our descent took us along a cinder path and brought us to the Stocktons' door.

"At least Shrevey got what's coming to him," Matt said. He was digging around in the refrigerator. "That louse."

"I wish it had been me," I added, "with the bat."

"Yeah," Matt said. "*Whack!*" The baseball bat had opened a crack in the back of Shrevey's head like the seam in a pomegranate. Blood had spattered dozens of lockers.

"I'da killed the bastard," I said.

But Ralph wasn't listening. He opened two Cokes. "That clown Prungle and his stupid lectures," he muttered. "Going on and on about the school." While he talked Ralph beat one fist on the counter rhythmically. His knuckles were scraped and starting to bruise, but he seemed unaware of them. He was saying, "Red Rock High this, Rockland Hotel that. You'd think the fight was every dimwit miner's business, not just between Shrevey and me." Ralph looked over at me. "Us," he added. He didn't notice his hand was bleeding from the pounding he was giving it. "Anyway," he said, "I don't give a hoot."

I drank my Coke slowly. I didn't want to get home. I had no stomach for one of Hansi's lectures. Schoolyard Fighting, Lecture Nine, Ralph called it. Subtitle: Behavior Unacceptable.

If you quarrel with miners' sons, Father had told us years ago, settle it like men, after classes, and with some dignity. You are boys now, but soon you'll be men, and men do not settle differences by fighting like dogs. And the like.

Mother had interrupted him at this point. We were all surprised. "And you'll tear your clothes," she said.

"That's not the point, that's not the point at all." We were sitting in the living room for this bit of moral instruction, Father and Mother in chairs and Ralph and me on the sofa. I was maybe five, and had been told to listen carefully. Did Ralph have a bloody nose? In my lap I held a replica Euclid earth mover, bright yellow with huge black rubber wheels, which I spun as Father talked.

"Only in Italy do men fight like this. And you know by now what the world thinks of Italians." Father looked from Ralph to me and back to Ralph to make sure we understood. "You want a reputation like that?"

I knew we didn't and was about to say so, but before I could, Ralph asked, "What if someone else starts?" He was a thinker even at the age of seven — always a step ahead.

Father blinked. He hesitated, and Mother answered for him. "Turn the other cheek. The Christian thing to do."

That was ten years ago, but I smiled recalling it as we stood in the Stocktons' kitchen drinking Cokes. My parents. Their advice was so old-fashioned. So much about them was. Sure, Hansi had a zoot suit in the latest cut and Tina a Persian lamb's wool coat. But their morals, their manners, the punishments they meted out for misbehavior. Even the supper-time lectures when Father dispensed advice with the same certainty as he passed around the plates of chops and mashed potato. They were from another time and place. Not Red Rock in the brazen fifties: pedal pushers, pageboys, rattail combs, Elvis. Still, they meant well.

Ralph said to Matt, "And of course Prissy Prungle had to call the old man at work."

"Of course," said Matt. "The drip."

Ralph said, "I can hear him now: 'Mr. Frudel, we hate to bother you during business hours, but we thought you'd want to hear it from us first.' Prungle. Such an ass-kisser."

When we finished our Cokes we made our way home slowly, dragging our feet in the gravel. They raised puffs in the air like ghosts, and our sneakers and pant cuffs became coated in red dust.

On the doorstep Mother was waiting, and when she saw my face she kneaded her apron in her fists. She had been expecting this — or worse. We'd heard her whispering to Father about miners' sons. She understood them better than he did — the schoolyard bullying, the name calling, the beatings. Hadn't she predicted that someday someone would die on the schoolyard?

She touched my cheek as we mounted the stairs, but I brushed her hand away. (The first of many slights I inflicted on her, a boy eager to be a man.) Above my left eye a bruise as big as a baseball puffed out. Blood had matted my hair. But I set my jaw on taking it like a man. I saw that Mother wanted to take me in her arms, to comfort me the way she had when I came home from kindergarten with my crayons broken. Instead she whispered, "Father's waiting."

We marched into the living room, no longer boys but men, our pursed lips seemed to say, the rhythmic thud of our shoes on the hardwood floors. Beyond the tears of women. Beyond softness and confessions and apologies. We were Hansi Frudel's sons.

He said: "It's not I mind about Shrevey Russell, the pig-eyed son of a pig-eyed father, if there was ever one who needed straightening out. Bill Russell with his union bull — Pah. He deserves what he gets. But boys, in school. Then to attack one of the teachers."

He paused but he was not waiting for us to respond. In these sessions he did the talking and we listened with hands in laps. He was waiting for what he'd said to sink in. To make an impression. I was trying not to think of the word *bullshit*. Father had nearly uttered it, and I was fighting back the giggles. If they got out, I'd really be in for it. Ralph was studying his shoes. Drops of blood had hardened on their toes. Was this my blood or Shreve's? Or Ralph's?

"I'm not pleased with you, boys," Father continued. "Not pleased at all. You disgrace yourselves. You disgrace our family. Think of your mother. Think of her shopping at Safeway tomorrow. The shame of having hooligans for sons."

This was the word Father saved for the worst moments, *hooligans*. It was what the vets at the Legion called men who'd lost control in Europe. Men who raped women, who got blood-lust, who lacked restraint. Hooligans. Father had a lecture about this, too.

"It is your behavior," he said, turning his gaze to Ralph, "that shocks me. This one" — he nodded briefly toward me — "I can understand how he might do something stupid. But an older brother, one who is supposed to set an example . . . who's supposed to have more between the ears."

Ralph cleared his throat.

"You have something to say, maybe?"

"No, sir." Ralph ran one hand and then the other through his hair, ruffling his rooster tail. A prelude to rash action.

"No, I should hope. For such behavior there is no excuse." Father stood and went to the window. Past his head I

55

saw the willows the town council had planted along the boulevard of our street and beyond their wispy tips puffs of black smoke belching from the stacks at the mines. Father had been chafing the boils on the back of his neck. He muttered, "And for a boy of such promise. Do you know what it meant for a boy in my day to get a scholarship?" He faced Ralph. "Such a distinction. Such an honor to the family. And to squander it in a schoolyard scrap. Pah." He fiddled with his tie. "Prungle says you've let them all down." He waited, but again not for an answer. "And over what? Some silly girl?"

"It was not over a girl," Ralph said between clenched teeth, and when he touched his rooster tail, I caught my breath.

Father tilted forward. "So now the wiseguy speaks," he said, challenging Ralph to say more so he could really let him have it. His eyes fixed each of us in turn. I squirmed on the Naugahyde sofa and marveled at Ralph's daring. That anyone would talk back to Father. He asked, "If not girls, what then?"

"Nothing," Ralph mumbled.

"No, please go on. Speak, boy of genius IQ and baseball bats."

I stammered, "He mocked you, Dad, he said — "

Father's eyes widened in sudden knowing. "What?" he asked, his voice cold and level like the winter wind. "Said what?"

Before I could open my mouth Ralph blurted, "He called Dickie a fairy."

"What?" Father asked, incredulous. He looked from one of us to the other. He wasn't fooled. But his will was up against Ralph's and he sensed he was about to lose.

"What?" he asked again, feigning control and the certainty of being answered.

He waited, but Ralph would not reply, and when Father was certain he would not, he turned his gaze to me, already knowing it was futile to hope to pry from the disciple what he could not get from the master. His face turned bright red. His own sons refusing him. It was too much. He could not believe it. Fighting in the schoolyard was one thing, but

56

refusing to answer, adding insolence to defiance. It was too much.

Perhaps that's why he said what he did, and why Mother, listening in the kitchen, caught her breath. "We'll see," he hissed between set teeth, wheeling and striding out of the room. "We'll see, Ralph my boy." And even I, the younger brother, the slow one, again studying the blood on Ralph's shoe, knew from the tone he meant we'll see Mister Wiseguy, Mister California Institute of Technology, when they take your scholarship away, how you'll come begging. We'll see what you say then, bright boy.

Eleven

That night I found myself listening outside the door of my parents' bedroom when we were all supposed to be asleep. I was not eavesdropping. I was, if anything, afraid to be there, my fat feet turning blue with cold on the hallway tiles. No, I was not eavesdropping. The things my parents did behind closed doors frightened me:

sex things, when the bedsprings groaned

quarrels with strained voices rising

conversations about Ralph and me.

So blame my small bladder for the fact I was there at all, stranded between my need to pee and the earnest tones of my parents' voices.

It was past midnight. I'd been lying in bed thinking about Ralph. After supper in his room he'd made me watch as he stuck one of Mother's giant sewing needles into his wrist. Blood spurted, arced down to the floor. He did it a second time. He didn't flinch. The third time he fixed his eyes on mine as he punched the needle into the white flesh. My mouth went dry.

That was hours ago, but my knees were still trembling, so I eased out of bed and turned the doorknob stealthily, then stalked along the hallway, feeling the cold floor turning my toes to ice. My heart pounded in my fat chest. Just as I reached my parents' bedroom I heard my name and stopped dead in my tracks.

"That it should be Dickie to blame," Father was saying.

"Hansi." My mother spoke between sobs. "Not blame."

"He isn't to blame?" Father's voice rose and then abruptly fell. Mother must have shushed him. He whispered, "Prungle says — "

"Blame isn't the point."

"What is the point then?"

Mother blew her nose. In the long silence following I swallowed hard, certain they could hear my breathing, my pounding heart. I heard someone crossing the floor toward me. I pressed myself to the wall and prayed.

"Did you see his face?" Mother's voice was under control now. "Did you look at your son when he came through the front door? Bruises round his eyes? Blood matted in his hair? When I washed it later gashes as long as your thumb."

"Tina, this is not the point."

"If the murder of my son isn't the point, I want to know what is. Because I've told you, Hansi, how many times have I said, miners' kids are animals. Trash. They'll kill someone down at that school one of these days and if it should be your son . . . if it should be Dickie . . ."

"Hush." Hansi sighed, and I heard him punching his pillow. "Hush now or you'll start having nightmares again."

In the silence I was tempted to scoot to the bathroom, but something held me there. Finally Mother said, "We should have sent them to private school."

"On what we make at the hardware? The very idea."

"Some things money can't buy." The bed creaked, footsteps started across the floor, and my heart leapt into my mouth. I tried moving but my feet stuck to the tiles. I searched for explanations, excuses. But in a moment the bedsprings creaked again and Mother blew her nose.

I retreated a few steps toward my bedroom. But my bladder was bursting, my feet aching with cold. I envied Ralph his warm bed and deaf ears.

My own ears ached from cuts and bruises. Mother had bathed them with epsom salts before daubing on Mercurochrome with a cotton-tipped stick. There were other injuries. My jaw made grinding sounds when I chewed. Hearing them over supper, Ralph looked at me slyly and smiled — the conspiratorial smile of brothers in trouble together. And my ears rang with the pitch of struck crystal, so I had trouble hearing what my parents were saying.

Mother asked Father, "So it's settled then?"

"If anything ever is settled with teachers. Today they blow this way, tomorrow that. You remember how they fussed about Dickie at first, but then when he did not live up to their tests . . ."

"Yesterday Ralph was on top of the world. We all were."

"Yesterday he hadn't half killed a boy. Struck a teacher."

"And the scholarship?"

"Gone. The scholarship is voted by the faculty and Prungle says they can't give thousands of dollars to a boy who breaks the school rules about fighting, who takes the law into his own hands."

"They take themselves very seriously."

"Like I say, school teachers."

"What they really mean is he's too proud to apologize."

"Prungle didn't say that."

"But he meant it, didn't he?" Mother's voice was insistent now. "He should have said it because that's the real reason Ralph's not going to get the money. Because he had the guts to stand up to the principal. Because he has backbone."

"Yes. He said the boy was pigheaded."

"Pigheaded? Did he say the word Kraut?"

"Tina."

"Or Nazi?"

"Oh lord."

"No, he wouldn't, would he, with his nice-smelling English wife. He wouldn't bother with that little truth, would he?" Mother blew her nose again. "Oh, how it must have irked them that the great scientist was coming here not to see the Fitzgerald boy, or even Matt Stockton. No, the great scientist was coming from NASA with his retinue of young geniuses to see Ralph Frudel, son of German DPs. Of Krautheads."

"We're Canadian, Tina. It's two generations."

"Tell them that when they look down their noses at Women's Auxiliary as if I was responsible for Hitler. Tell that to Mrs. Prungle at her bake sales where everybody gets invited except me because my strudel might contaminate them with some Nazi disease."

"Tina, don't excite yourself." Father shifted on the bed and I couldn't hear what he said. Something about nightmares.

"They must have been just waiting for an excuse to take that scholarship away. Fighting in the school! Do you think this would happen if it was the Fitzgerald boy? Or Matt Stockton? English children of English parents?"

Father shifted in bed again and I believe he put his arms around my mother, comforting her, because what she said next was lost. Muffled.

I inched closer to their door, straining to hear, I blush to confess.

Father said, "There's always the money in the trust."

And Mother, "You don't mean that — not really."

"Yes." Father sighed. "He is our son when all is said and done."

"Is that what you want?"

"I know it's what you want. Isn't it?"

"But this afternoon — when you talked to the boys."

Father cleared his throat. "Tina," he said. "You know how I detest pride. It was the one thing about army officers . . ." In the silence he left I heard Ralph snoring. "Both our boys have fine qualities, many gifts and talents, and they will be good men when they grow up. But Ralph . . . Ralph has so many dark moods — impulses, ambitions, rages. Most of all pride."

"I know," whispered Mother.

"And sometimes . . . sometimes I lose control when he challenges me like that. He's too strong, too willful."

"Too much like you," Mother said. "Correct?"

"Yes." Father laughed at that, a brief snort of a laugh followed by a sigh. "Too much like me."

And the rest I didn't hear. Mother's voice was muffled again in crying. I used the cover of her sobs to scoot along the hall, feet frozen hard as steel but heart soft with the goodness of parents, past their door.

So. There was the trust, hadn't Father said so? And all the fears I'd stored in my ghostly heart were nothing, all the misery Ralph and I had shared after supper in his room when we cursed California turned to dust, when we cursed Shrevey Russell, Prissy Prungle, and even our own father. When we cursed Werner von Braun. When Ralph drew blood from his wrist and smiled wickedly as it pooled on the floor at our feet. When everything was turning to ashes there was what Ralph and I had never reckoned on: Hansi's trust.

Twelve

They should not have been surprised to find him that way the next morning. They should never have been surprised by anything Ralph did. He was blue-faced and cold. His straw-blond hair stuck up from his scalp in a weird curl, forming a question mark. No, it did not surprise me. No more than taking a bat to Shrevey Russell did, or piercing his own flesh with a sewing needle. Hadn't they noticed the mood swings? If they'd asked, I would have told them what Ralph was capable of.

But they didn't ask.

They weren't blind, so what was it? Maybe they were merely following the wisdom of the fifties when everything except war was considered a passing phenomenon, best left to run its trivial course. What a decade. Do you remember? This Too Will Pass might have been our motto. All in Good Time. Yes, the tranquilized fifties, when psychology was a joke and Containment and Consolidation our bywords. The cold war, they called it. Certainly everyone's heart was frozen — and most brains numb. That's why no one noticed Ralph's mood swings, or intervened to protect him from himself.

Perhaps you think I'm unfair to my parents? They had other things on their minds. Father was brooding about layoffs at the mines and preoccupied with breaking the trust he'd set up in Mother's name so as to protect the family if the hardware store went bankrupt and the creditors came after his assets. And Mother? She fretted about her recurring nightmares, her lost baby, the fact that Aunt Ellen was now taking cobalt treatments and her hair was falling out. Mother was convinced she'd get leukemia, too, and she pictured herself in a hospital bed with tubes running out her nose.

So that night after Ralph had clubbed Shrevey Russell they probably weren't thinking about how he felt. Like responsible parents of the fifties they had talked it over and were satisfied they were doing the right thing, breaking the trust to send Ralph to Cal Tech. It was good. It was noble. They must have fallen asleep happy, thinking in a few days — when enough time had passed for Ralph to appreciate their generosity and had learned a lesson about pride — they would tell him the good news.

As usual, he was a step ahead of them. He was in torment when he went to bed, and when he woke in the night, he probably punished himself with thoughts of his misbegotten future. It added up to a big zero. Prungle was right. He'd lost everything: career, fame, money, women. The red Mercedes with wing doors. He got up and prowled the house, touching the cold tiles but feeling nothing. Feeling the nothing all around him. The nothing ahead of him, the nothing he'd become. One big zero, as he would have said.

It was a warm night, autumn according to the calendar, but with summer warmth in the midnight air. Perhaps Ralph saw an irony there. The tree branches in the back yard were tossed by breezes and the moon shone in at the kitchen window. It was round and bright. It dappled the wooden bench at the bottom of the yard, the bench Father and I had built several summers earlier.

Ralph stood at the kitchen window. He poured some orange juice and left the dirty glass on the counter next to Mother's scouring pads. To me, anyway, this showed he'd got up with some other intent than suicide. Or no intent at all. Just restless, maybe, in his troubled way. Padding the floor of the empty house past midnight. It was not unusual for him.

The idea must have come to him as he prowled the house, torturing himself with thoughts of failure. Like I say, he took every setback hard. And I knew he would not deliberately drink a glass of California Golden Orange Juice before the final act. Not even Ralph was that cynical.

I like to think it was while he was drinking the juice that the full irony struck him. Yes. He was darkly impulsive.

Of course he had the family history to draw on. Uncle Stefan dead at twenty-six, hurling his embarrassment about a hearing aid into the path of an on-coming Edsel. Have I mentioned two cousins who killed themselves before they were twenty? The first was a shy girl we'd both danced with at a family wedding, attractive in an elfin way. She shot herself in her bedroom on the third floor of a rambling house with a shotgun. No note. No explanation. "A bad business," said Father at the funeral. "The blood." Maybe that's why the other cousin chose drowning. He leapt off a city bridge and floated to the surface miles downstream weeks later. He left a note: a long misspelled note addressed to no one in particular and the whole world in general, citing nothing personal for what he'd done but the sins of man against man — wars, pollution, crime. He included a newspaper clipping about starvation in Africa. Several years his junior, Ralph had spent weekends with him at his home in Toronto, going to movies, chatting up girls. At the funeral Ralph confided to me, "He was aces." And then added enigmatically, "It couldn't have been a girl."

About suicide Father said this: "The most selfish act there is. Somebody takes their life when thousands — no, millions — have fought and died to secure that life, have sacrificed blood and guts so someone in a fit of ego can make a soapbox gesture. What does it all amount to? I'll tell you what it amounts to: to this childish cry — look at me, everybody, look at my suffering. Pah. Think of the dead in Russia. The skeletons we freed from the death camps at Belsen and Dachau. Do you know how people scratched to hang on to their miserable existences in the most wretched circumstances — beatings, starvation, forced labor? Rape even. Ask them about self-pity. Ask them about suicide. They believed in the dignity of life. You see?"

We nodded our heads but Ralph did not look at it this way, and neither did I. Ralph lived in an all-or-nothing world where if you didn't get what you wanted, you raged, you lashed out, you threw tantrums. Around our house he was as famous for his tantrums as for his marks of a hundred on math tests. And what was suicide except the ultimate tantrum?

I saw it different from Ralph. I'd looked around and seen there was not that much to be in a rage about. Nothing so bad you'd kill yourself over it. Sure, life was a game of snakes and ladders, you never knew where the next toss of the dice would land you, how bad you'd fall. Here's what I mean. Mrs. Adreta, two doors down the street, died from cancer of the liver, leaving her husband to raise six children, the Oliphant boy at school had crossed eyes, Mr. Hansen a cleft palate, the Childress twins born with defective kidneys, a car drove over Albert Shield's foot, Matt Stockton's mother took electroshock therapy for nerves, I was overweight, Ralph depressive, and Father drank too much. It was a surprise sometimes that anyone got through life unscathed. And maybe no one really did. That's what life was. Pain. But it didn't mean it was all bad. Not at all. There was the bright sun every morning, the crack of a bat on a ball, the smile on Father's face when he'd done a good job, the taste of crackling cold Pepsi. Yes. That, anyway, is how I saw it. So, in a way, I agreed with Father.

"You see," he repeated, continuing his lecture, "when some matron swallows a bottle of pills because her chiseling lover dumped her I just get sick. Feh. Don't tell me about the nobility of suicide. It's egotism plain and simple. Egotism, boys."

Ralph and I listened to this lecture with straight faces, hands in laps, but afterwards we huddled together and said in unison: "What the hell was that all about?" Ralph was troubled by this lecture but when I called it "Our side or suicide?" he laughed and rushed off to tell Matt Stockton.

After the cousin's bloody bedroom you knew Ralph would not choose the shotgun method. He might have considered death by drowning: it had the advantage of being clean. And in grade twelve he studied T. S. Eliot's famous *Wasteland*, so he knew the reference to the drowned Phoenician. It was a mile to the Pickerel River, though, and Ralph was in the grip of impulse.

That impulsiveness saved his life.

He went to the garage. Dressed only in pyjamas, he sat in the driver's seat of Hansi's Meteor and started the engine. What he'd read about toxic gases would have told him carbon monoxide would first make him dizzy and then giddy. His eyes would smart and he'd want to rub them. Then came the desire for sleep. Just lean forward over the wheel for support, but not on the horn. Close the eyes and drift off into a better world. No more arguments about Cal Tech, no more fighting with Hansi.

And that's how Father found him. The way he told it later, he knew something was wrong when he saw the side door of the garage banging to and fro in the early-morning breeze. He went out in his slippers, coffee mug in hand. When he looked inside he was overcome by haze. He choked and coughed. He called out *Tina* in the way of married people when there's danger and urgency.

He dragged Ralph from behind the wheel and slapped his face, already blue with death. Ralph's hair was sticking up crazily and there was a tight-lipped grin on his lips, mocking maybe.

In Europe Father had revived men who'd been stunned by explosions. He'd given first aid to the wounded. Twice he'd been cited for valorous conduct and at Christmas still he received cards of thanks from two vets whose lives he had saved. He dragged Ralph into the grass where he flipped him on his back and spread-eagled him before starting artificial respiration. Christ, he thought, not now, not this when . . . He was not thinking of sacrifice then. He was thinking of the sarcastic words he'd hurled at Ralph in the living room. He wept. He shouted for Tina to phone the ambulance. And he did what he had always done when one of his buddies was dying on his hands in Europe. He prayed.

Thirteen

Red Rock General was located on the far side of town, just off the main road leading to the mines. It served the usual purposes — tending to hemorrhoids, pregnancies, and scraped knees. But it was also there for the miners — men with broken legs, electrical shock, crushed hands, severed arms, heat exhaustion, injured backs. Wrestling hematite from the earth is dangerous work. Andrew McGuire was in charge of the hospital. An alcoholic, as well as brother of the banker, Andrew McGuire wisely surrounded himself with a team of competent nurses.

Ralph opened his swollen eyes and saw a white ceiling with high bright lights. He also saw the reassuring smile of a blond nurse. He'd been unconscious for three days. The white ceiling reflected the white walls which reflected the white ceiling. Ralph's eyes hurt. He blinked. The nurse was pleasant to look at, but not the walls and ceiling. He shut his eyes.

Tina was at the cafeteria getting a cup of tea. When she returned Ralph was out again, but the nurse told her he was on the road to recovery. Tina looked sad. The nurse told her Ralph would be out now for another long stretch. Tina held her cup in her lap and sat perched on the edge of a chair, studying her son's face.

It had been a long three days of watching, waiting, and praying. She knew the pattern in the floor tiles in this room well. She did not know the names of the other five patients crowded into the room Ralph shared with them. The woman next to Ralph had a portable transistor radio. Tina had heard the same news reports dozens of times: the Russians had launched a rocket into space called *Sputnik*. Vacationing in

Florida, the President assured the American public that the U.S. would soon have a man in space and would land one on the moon within the decade. Werner von Braun's name was not mentioned. There was a bureaucratic snarl over refugees fleeing Hungary. Hurricane Bertha was bearing in on the Gulf State. Grace Kelly had been seen at a party with Prince Ranier of Monaco.

Tina stood and studied Ralph. His fingers twitched holding the hem of the hospital sheet. From above, his cheeks seemed washed-out, his skin translucent. Both Tina's sons puckered their lips and made popping noises while they slept. At the hospital Ralph breathed irregularly, gasping air, not yet fully confident of life. Beneath his eyes were dark pouches, the same as when he'd had chicken pox. But he was alive. Tina stooped and kissed his brow. It was hot and moist. She felt the embarrassment of a mother who kisses her grown son, and she stepped back quickly. How many years had it been since she'd kissed him publicly?

She went to the mirror over the washstand and studied her own face: deeper lines in the cheeks and brows than she liked to see. She touched the dark pouches under her eyes that had developed from not sleeping — and from worrying. She splashed her face with cold water and dried it on paper towels. She straightened a line of lipstick that was wearing thin as her nerves.

Where was Hansi? An hour ago she'd phoned him at the store, and he said he'd come as soon as he finished the day's receipts. Money, money, money. She should phone and tell him the news. Ralph was conscious. But what if he woke again when she was out of the room phoning? That would be an opportunity missed. Tina pursed her lips. She'd wait an hour before calling.

Hansi was taking it tough. During the first hours he was cool and efficient, giving instructions to the attendants who met them at the hospital doors, supplying information to the nurse at the front desk. He had rolled up his shirt sleeves the way working men do and discarded his tie. The man of action. He conferred with Dr. McGuire in hushed tones, telling him

69

how he discovered the body. In the waiting room he held Tina's hand and assured her with anecdotes from the battle-field. His voice soothed her.

Hours passed. In the evening when the halls fell silent, when the last visitor had left and patients slept, Hansi shared a quiet hour with her over a bowl of soup in the cafeteria. He was there when they wheeled Ralph from the operating room, one strong hand on Dr. McGuire's elbow. He was there into the early-morning hours when they charted Ralph's breathing on the monitors and said he was out of danger.

That was at the hospital. When they got home he started to unravel. He went straight to the cupboard where he stored the liquor and poured a water glass of whiskey. "Why me?" he asked no one in particular. Tina was fixing a pot of tea. "What did I do, Tina?" he asked, not expecting an answer from anything except the tumbler before him. "Where did I go wrong?"

He sat at the kitchen table with his bare elbows sticking out. He finished his whiskey and then stared at the residue in the bottom of the tumbler. Tears formed in the corners of his eyes but he brushed them away with his knuckles.

Tina sat with him to drink her tea. She said, "If it was Dickie . . ." She stirred a lump of sugar around her cup, clinking the spoon on the rim. The beginnings of a smile crinkled her mouth. "But he doesn't have the temperament. Ralph's flair for drama."

Hansi poured a second water glass of whiskey. His hand shook when he raised it to drink. That hand had pointed a flame-thrower at a peasant in Italy. Why had he thrown a grenade at the Canadian troops liberating them? Hansi had asked himself that every day since it happened. He had watched a firing squad shoot deserters, three young privates from Quebec who had been conscripted and tried to row across an Italian lake into Switzerland one night. Everything about the war seemed to come back to him colored red. The peasant had run from a burning barn, the deserters were shot against a red brick wall with green vines growing on it. Yes,

Hansi had seen violence up close. But this was different. This was his own flesh and blood.

When he poured a third tumbler of whiskey, Tina said, "That's the second bottle this week." He looked from the glass to the bottle as if they had nothing to do with him. But he didn't say anything. He retreated into the silence of his own thoughts where whiskey dulled the ache of falling sales, of mortgages, of foreclosure dates. And now this: a son with brains enough to build the atomic bomb but who lacked the strength to face one failure. One little setback.

Hansi shook his head as if waking from a trance. He took out his pocketknife and dug under his nails and brooded:

How long would it be before they lost the store?

Where would they go, and what would they do?

Why was everything coming apart at once?

The third glass always went easier than the second. And the fourth easier than the third. Tina propped her chin in her hands and stared past Hansi's shoulder. The tea was bitter to her taste. Hansi's eyes refused to meet hers. She wept and the tears formed rivulets and ran into the corners of her mouth and tasted salty. She wanted to say, "Hansi, I'm scared." She ached to fall into his arms like she did when they were first married. To cry, "Hansi, what can we do?" knowing he would have an answer. But instead she stared into space, silent.

He took her hand and turned it over in his. "What did I do?" he asked. "Where did I go wrong?" He was thinking about the trust money, about Ralph's tuition, about his angry words. Only a few hours ago they were happy. He was also thinking about layoffs and strikes.

"We," Tina said. She stood at the sink composing herself. She dumped the tea from the pot and rinsed it quickly under the tap. "We have done nothing wrong."

Hansi studied her over his glass. "Yes," he whispered. "We."

Tina said, "I need sleep."

After she was gone, Hansi poured the last of the whiskey. There was not much left in the water glass: two long swallows. He sat looking at the empty bottle, resisting thoughts of mortgages and foreclosures: if the damn mines hadn't expanded so fast, if all the businesses in town hadn't been swept along on the wave of progress, giddy with greed. And then the cutbacks. Who could have guessed it would happen so fast? Hansi thought about the boom-and-bust cycle of capitalism, about trust funds, scholarships, and tuition to the California Institute of Technology. And a boy too weak to face one small setback. He tried not to think about how he was losing his business and his firstborn son. He had no idea he might soon lose his beloved wife.

Fourteen

The woman in the bed next to Ralph's listened to pop music: Patsy Cline, the Andrews Sisters. "Honeycomb" was still a big hit. When the news came on she turned the volume up and cocked one ear toward the set. "Imagine the Russians sending a rocket into space," she said to Tina. Like most people, she was fascinated by *Sputnik*. "They've got the leg up on us there." She shook her head. "Our scientists are dopes."

Waiting at Ralph's bedside, Hansi and Tina exchanged furtive glances. Then Tina stepped closer to catch the woman's words over the radio's static. The woman had a hatchet face and a large mole on her chin. When she leaned forward to speak, she winced, cradling pain in her stomach. She was a chain smoker: butts filled the ashtray on the night table.

"My name's Frudel," Tina said. "Tina. And that's Hansi."

"It's my legs." The woman suddenly pulled aside the blankets covering her legs. "Look." She wiggled one thin leg over the side. From the knee down it was a sickly yellow and blue. The leg had no calf muscle. It looked like it had been cut away.

Tina put her hand on her stomach.

"It's all right for him," the woman went on, indicating Ralph with her head. "He's on the way back. He's recovering."

Tina looked from one bed to the other. "We were scared."

"No need there." The woman blew a cloud of smoke into the air as she spoke. "But I'm going the other way."

Hansi looked away from her. He twiddled his thumbs.

The woman fumbled with the volume on the radio,

turned it higher rather than lower, and scowled at it before continuing. "Cancer," she shouted. They listened to the weather report. More rain. From the night table she produced a package of Lucky Strikes. "Have one?" Tina shook her head. The woman found a lighter. "Myrtle," she said past the blue flame.

"Tina," repeated Tina inanely.

"Myrtle Dobson. Me and the old man run the Highway Esso." Tina had heard of her: a woman who pumped gas, whose children ran free on the streets in tattered and dirty clothes. Catholic, Tina guessed from the cross dangling from the chain round her neck.

Tina said, "It's quiet in here." She stood at the foot of Myrtle's bed, clutching her handbag against her stomach.

"Crazy place for cancer to start," Myrtle said, "the ankles. Makes me something of an oddity round the place." She lit her cigarette and wiped the air in front of her face with a thin and fragile hand. "But just as deadly."

Tina studied Myrtle's hands: scabs on the back and raw spots like on her sister Ellen's. The bones almost poked through the skin. Emaciated, Tina thought. That word came to mind whenever she thought of Ellen. These women looked drained and defeated. It suddenly struck Tina that's how she had looked in the mirror over the washstand: hollow cheeks and pouches beneath the eyes. She had the tell-tale signs. First her sister Ellen was dying, and now this Myrtle. Would she be next?

Ellen had written almost as soon as she got back to Toronto. She'd started the cobalt treatments. Twice a week until the cancer reached remission, she wrote. They didn't hurt, not after the first bit, and the pain was dull and remote, like the gnaw of a dentist's drill. She'd had a few momentary blackouts, though, and some nights when she didn't sleep at all after the treatments. She was losing tufts of hair already. But she did not have much pain.

Tina shuddered to think of it. She'd only been in the hospital to have children. She'd never been seriously ill, never faced prolonged suffering. Not really. Ellen's accounts of her cancer treatments horrified Tina. From the time she was a child she'd been terrified of disease. When she was a girl diphtheria had swept the country, and Tina had seen friends sicken and die. Then came tuberculosis with its coughing fits, its hot compresses, its sanatoriums. Her boys had been lucky to escape polio, though they had had to get the booster shots in the arms. And now there was cancer. People were falling over dead from it every day. My God, she prayed, don't let it be me. But she knew praying was as futile as the hot compresses had been.

There was the vomiting, for one. She dreaded getting up in the morning because she knew it was coming. Spasms twisting her insides, they left her feeling shaken for the rest of the day. Lately she'd noticed black flecks coming up, too, making a dark stream that whirled into the toilet basin and turned the water pink when she flushed.

"You okay?" Myrtle asked. Her glazed eyes studied Tina over her smoldering cigarette. "You look green round the gills."

Tina nodded toward Ralph's bed. "I've been up all night."

Myrtle lit one cigarette off another. Her lips trembled as she waited for the flame to catch. "Me too."

What Tina wanted was a cup of strong tea. She imagined a pot of Irish Breakfast with three lumps of sugar and no milk. The hospital cafeteria served little tin pots that dribbled and bags of Orange Pekoe that turned bitter with steeping. She wanted strong brew. Behind her she heard Hansi breathing, keeping vigil over Ralph's bed. She pulled up a chair and sat to one side of Myrtle where the smoke from the cigarettes wouldn't bother her.

Myrtle asked, "Your only boy?"

"Our eldest," Tina said. "Older," she corrected herself.

"I've got six." Myrtle shook her head and smiled. Her teeth were crooked and stained brown. "Always getting into something. Trouble mostly." She sank back in the pillows and smoke escaped through her teeth toward the ceiling. She asked, "Accident?"

Tina shifted on her chair. This was the moment she'd

dreaded. What could you say? How could you tell a stranger your son went into the garage and turned on the car motor? A Catholic? She looked over her shoulder for Hansi. He was gone.

Tina left a long silence and then asked, "How long has it been — since you first found out?"

"Three years," Myrtle said matter-of-factly. She pulled the blankets up over her leg, covering it again. "Though it seems like all of my life." She took a long drag on her cigarette and studied the ceiling. "One day you're in high school learning about the coureurs de bois and the next you're pregnant with your third child and the next they take you into the hospital for cancer. You know?" She shrugged the way people did whenever they were cornered. "You ask yourself, where did it all go? What does it add up to?"

Tina was wishing she had gone to the cafeteria with Hansi. She longed for a cup of tea.

"It started in the ankles," Myrtle was saying. "And then moved up. First the calves of my legs. They look like they've been taken out with an ice cream scoop, don't they?" The image pleased her. She smiled and looked toward Ralph's bed. She repeated "ice cream" under her breath. She added weakly, her voice dropping suddenly, "Then it went into the stomach. I've had six operations on my stomach."

Tina liked Myrtle. She was straightforward. She faced up to her lot in life. She smiled. Maybe, Tina thought, that came from having a large family. Or from knowing you were dying. She asked, "And how long did all this take?"

"Well, like I said, the whole thing's been going on for three years. This last bit maybe eighteen months." Myrtle finished her cigarette and stubbed it out in the ashtray on her night table. "I'll tell you this. Once it gets into the stomach it's hell."

Three years! Eighteen months! The numbers were appalling. Tina could not tolerate the idea of suffering. And yet Myrtle had endured this pain for years. And she could smile. Tina was in awe of her. To fight a disease for so long. Tina had the impression from newspapers and radio that cancer killed suddenly. But Myrtle had been fighting to live for longer than some wars lasted. The woman with the bad teeth and wild kids everyone gossiped about had endured. She might even triumph. Tina experienced a rush of hope.

"Of course," Myrtle continued, "the doctors always say the longer you hang on the better. Experiments are going on round the clock. Tomorrow could bring the breakthrough." She smiled thinly as if she knew she was telling the kind of story you tell children to make things easier for them, to hide the painful facts. "The miracle drug, the miracle cure." She looked very tired suddenly. She lay back and closed her eyes. "Hard to believe," she mumbled.

"I believe it." Tina found she was holding Myrtle's bony hand and squeezing it with conviction. "I believe it," she repeated. "And you must too."

Fifteen

At first they wouldn't let me go to him. "Dickie," Father said at the kitchen table that first night, "he'll get worked up if he sees you. He's in such a state . . ." He clamped his hands on the back of a chair so hard his knuckles turned white. And Mother looking up from a cup of tea signaled me to sit with her at the table where she poured a mug from the pot and stirred in the sugars for me. Squeezed my hand in hers. Muttered something about Ralph's high-strung nature.

But I was not taken in. I didn't for a moment believe Ralph would be upset if he saw me. No more than I believed what they said had happened on the morning Father found him in the garage. "An accident," Mother told me when I came out on the stoop in my pyjamas, following their urgent voices and fussing about. "Ralph's had an accident with the car." Not only did this seem unlikely, but Mother's voice cracked the way it always did when she lied, when she tried to shield us from awful truths. Why do parents do that?

While father talked I butted my fists together and swore under my breath. I thought if anything was going to upset him it was seeing them with their set smiles and blank eyes. That would plunge anyone into depression. I, on the other hand, could bring life to his face. Maybe start the swing back the other way. I was Dickie, after all, the devoted kid brother, the joker. But I was packed off to school as if it was an ordinary day — ordinary except Mother gave me an Eat More to have between classes and messed with my hair before I left.

In class I glanced around every time someone came in

the room, expecting it to be a call to Ralph's bedside. Prissy Prungle avoided me in the hall. Badger Mendez looked away when I put up my hand in class. Talk among students suddenly stilled when I rounded corners, kids seemed to be whispering things in the halls. Everyone knew something I didn't.

At lunch Mother told me to pay no mind to the kids at school. The sons and daughters of miners. She dismissed them with a wave of her hand. "Patsy Johnson's a stuck-up flirt and Shrevey the no-good son of a no-good father."

"How come they know and I don't?"

"They know nothing. They're just trying to get your goat." This was a favorite theme of hers, other kids were baiting me and I had to rise above their taunts — about being fat, for example.

Father sat beside me on the sofa and breathed whiskey in my face. "Do this for Ralph," he said. Show some backbone, he said. Rise above the gossip and rumors and name calling. He put his large hand on my shoulder, the hand with the family ring glinting blood red in the light. "A Frudel doesn't lower himself to the gutter with Shrevey Russell."

He made it seem like a contest where weasels like Shrevey gave in to rumors while real men stood on their dignity. It was comic book stuff, G.I. Joe, but I ate it up. Father talked about family loyalty, and the next day I sniffed when Shrevey's friends made snide comments about Ralph. Father spoke of grace under pressure and I imagined myself beside him in Europe, staring past blood and death, keeping a stiff upper lip, and I resolved to be worthy of his example. That was the second day.

"And tomorrow we'll all go to the hospital," Mother said, and gave me a Fat Emma and a Coke. Consolation prizes.

In the green hospital halls I smiled at the nurses and tried to look casual, but I took everything as an omen, saying to myself, if he sits up then I'll know I was right, he wants to talk to me, but if he turns his face away, then they were right and I was all wrong about brothers.

I was that nerved up.

Ralph lay on his back, toes pointed in the air. When he saw me he closed his eyes and I thought, they were right, it was a mistake for me to come, how could I believe there was anything special between us, the boy genius and the pinhead kid brother.

But he opened them immediately and said, "Long time no see." He added, "The walls are so bright. And the ceiling." I glanced around for a switch, but saw none. He read my mind. "They hide the switches in the basement," he said. "Along with the rubber chicken and the chemical cake. Central Control."

Mother stooped over and kissed his forehead. "Pooh," he sputtered, "dog lips." And he made a face.

I hadn't realized seeing him would make me feel so good. His eyes were dulled by drugs and his straw blond hair was unrulier than ever, but it was the same old Ralph, cracking jokes and looking devilish. A weight lifted from my shoulders. Since he'd gone to the hospital I'd convinced myself he was going to die. I'd pictured another scene at the graveyard, wearing the blazer and flannels.

I realized, too, how much my brother meant to me. Without him, my life was empty as the house once he was gone: no pillow fights, no singing "Heartbreak Hotel" at the tops of our lungs, no leaping out at Mother when she came home with the groceries. I even missed his black moods, moods when he flung books around or slammed the telephone on the floor after quarreling with a girl. However little I was able to console him in his moments of crisis, I missed our talks about his future and the way they opened up to me the great events beyond the pettiness of iron-stained Red Rock. He was more than my zany brother, he was my link to the larger world. The world of science and commerce and arts I heard of nightly on the CBC and had glimpsed for a moment in Mrs. Prungle's picture book. Toronto. The world I wanted to make my own.

This led to another realization, a grimmer one. I realized that I depended on Ralph to create and sustain my hopes for the future. Could it be the hollowness I felt in my stomach sprang more from selfishness than concern for Ralph? It was not a pleasant thought. And as I looked at him lying there, cheeks puffed with drugs, I felt monstrous shame. My only brother, my mentor and protector, lay within arm's reach of Death and I was fretting not for his immortal soul but about how it might ruin my chances of getting to Toronto. What a pathetic personality I had. I knew there were greater guilts in the world than this, but it was the lowest point to which I'd sunk in my undistinguished youth.

"Dickie, look here," he said. He motioned me to the beside. "Get a load of this card from Matt."

There were others, too, from school chums and family friends. Matt's pictured a parrot on a perch. *Get Well, Polly says,* the bubble over the parrot's head read. And inside, *You Crazy Cracker.*

When I bent to read it Ralph whispered in my ear, "How're they taking it?" He gripped my arm, that brown spot in his eye fixed on mine. Holding me, testing me. "Nia amant patrinoj?"

I shrugged and tried to look away, but there was no escaping his grip or that eye. "Tre bone," I said, smiling weakly. I tried to think of some lie to comfort him, but all I could come up with was the truth. "They're happy you made it through. We all are."

He'd leaned forward to catch my words and he sunk back suddenly. "Christ, Dickie," he said. "You don't know what it feels like lying here." His hand still gripped my arm.

"I hate hospitals."

"It's not that." He whispered so our parents couldn't hear. Bubbles of saliva formed on his lower lip. "I botched it. I botched it so bad." His voice had changed and I didn't want to hear what was coming next. "Lying here it's all I think about. Leaving that garage door open. La stulto!"

I squirmed. I wanted to be out of hearing range at the far side of the room — on the far side of the moon. "Don't," I said.

"Stop pretending," he hissed. He was leaning forward on one elbow and I smelled his sour breath on my face. "Just stop, will you?" When I didn't answer he went on, "You know what I mean, you've always known, but you've done a good job of faking it, you nearly fooled everyone with this fat-dumb-Dickie line. Nearly everyone." He held me there. "Look at them," he whispered, indicating our parents. "What a picture they make. The old Frudel stiff upper lip." His voice cracked and I thought he was going to laugh, one of those hideous laughs that made the hair on the back of my neck stand up.

He took a deep breath and licked his lower lip with a tongue lined by blue veins. He added, "Never mind. What they don't know is nothing's changed. Nenio. I'm still going to do it." He released my arm suddenly and gripped my wrist. "Get it, Dickie?"

Sixteen

Here was a predicament for the dutiful son and devoted kid brother. Ralph was not only taking me into his confidence, he was making me party to a second suicide attempt. I shook. I tried to say something but I had no words. What Ralph had done by speaking to me in secret was monstrous. At one stroke he had taken me into his confidence and pitted me against our parents. Me, the blundering kid brother.

We looked into each other's eyes for a moment and I knew my fate was sealed.

Then we left him for the night. We stood at the entrance to Red Rock General, Mother and Father two steps ahead of me, she with one hand hooked through his bent elbow. Then the full realization struck me. I groaned aloud. Mother turned an inquiring gaze on me. Father stopped talking. Standing there, the stench of ether fresh in my nostrils, the revolting odor of other people's sickness, I saw my parents as never before. Each looked shell-shocked: Mother with her haggard skin and eyes skittering from one thing to the next like a bird flitting among branches, Father trying to bear up, chin out in a parody of Teutonic self-control. The old Frudel fortitude. I saw them for the first time as small people. Dwarfed by the pillars of Red Rock General. Dwarfed by sickness and death.

Here was my dilemma. My duty lay with them. They'd taught me to believe in God, my country, and the family: the Holy Trinity of the fifties. They'd educated me to act like the great men. To do the right thing. Besides, they loved me unconditionally. And I knew it. To hold back Ralph's secret was a terrible betrayal.

On the other side was Ralph. Ralph, the manic brother I loved with a zeal beyond the ordinary devotion of the younger brother. Whose love I'd never quite been able to win — though I tried, God knows, on the playing fields, in the halls, at home, wherever my devotion might win his wayward heart. Yes, it was devotion. And more. Because it was not only love that bound me to him. There was also guilt, that singular mover in matters of the heart. I felt responsible for his predicament — his scholarship lost over my petty classroom quarrel with Shrevey Russell. And there was further guilt: I had not told him about our parents' intention of opening the trust to him. So on Ralph's account I faced guilt multiplied by guilt: guilt squared, Badger Mendez might have called it.

At fifteen, overweight, infatuated with baseball and terrified of girls, I had not realized life was so complicated. Or painful. So it was not just a childish jam, a schoolyard scrape that would pass with tears, or the scabbing of knees. It was my first full-blown adult crisis, complete with divided loyalties, guilt, love, misery, rage. And I was sweating, too. Everything I'd read about in novels but hadn't felt in my gut before.

So what did I do when facing my first adult dilemma there on the steps of Red Rock General, my parents looking back at me with expectation? I fell back on the habitual gestures of the younger brother, stammering something about how pale Ralph looked and shrugging my shoulders. The sky was dark from the effluence from the stacks at the mines and I studied it for a moment, as if expecting an answer to arrive from on high. Then I pretended I had coughed and I retreated into the silence parents mistake for teenage surliness. Father took out his polka-dot handkerchief and wiped his brow. Mother offered me a kleenex. But not even I, the shameless Dickie, believed the habitual shrug would resolve this dilemma. I was only hoping to buy the time necessary to think it through.

Father said, "He's okay now, Dickie, so don't go fretting yourself. He's got the Frudel fortitude." He placed his big hand on my shoulder. What a picture of family solidarity we made there on the bottom step of Red Rock General! And how my desperation deepened with each gesture my parents made to cement the family circle.

And on the way home we stopped at Iver's Diner for fish and chips, a treat because Father loved Mother's cooking and took us out to eat only once a year: on their wedding anniversary. His making the effort plunged me into greater anguish. My troubled conscience craved censure from my Father but he gave me instead breaded pickerel with Iver's special tartar sauce. My stomach turned on itself. I sat looking at my food, pushing chips around fish, but not eating. I would have choked.

When Mother asked was I ill, I could not look at her. She offered me a napkin and I felt worse taking it than a communicant accepting the sacred wafer without having first cleansed his soul. Her eyes met mine and my stomach knotted. I tried to speak but all I could do was blubber something about the fish being greasy.

And to myself I repeated Ralph's "what a picture they make" in order to harden my heart against them. Not that I had any difficulty finding things about them to dislike. There was Father's simple-minded philosophy of capitalism, amounting to little more than money grubbing. There was Mother's fear: by the standards of the fifties, especially the one Hansi taught us, contemptible. There was their gaudy middle-class junk: Naugahyde sofas, imitation Tiffany lamps, Arborite, Frigidaires. They were talking about buying a deep freeze.

But no matter how I despised the brittle self-control they'd wed to their bourgeois materialism, I could not hate them. There were the things we had shared: picnics at French Lake with ice cream and three-legged races on the grass, living-room talks about marriage and children, Pepsis at Hansi's Hardware after a day's work. No, I could not hate them when they'd given such love.

I wanted to open my mouth and speak the words that would warn them, but every time I prepared to, the image of Ralph lying in that hospital bed made me think better. His brown-spotted eye held me like a curse. The desperation in him was real. And he'd reached out to me the way younger brothers dream an older brother will: imploring. Testing, too. He'd whispered the words to me so there was no misunderstanding. I was his confidant, his confederate.

Yes, confederate. When he grabbed my wrist and whispered, "Get it, Dickie?" his tone added something else. Or maybe it was his eye. So fierce with the manic intensity I'd grown to love and fear. With all the power he could muster — and he knew the power he held over me — he implicated me in his terrible scheme. He didn't say much but the unspoken words were more important than those he spoke. The unspoken words were these: and I expect you to keep your trap shut, to know all but say nothing. To help me.

When we got home I took a walk in the hills, but the birds seemed to have left, there were no sounds except the distant rumble of blasting at the mines. From the hills I could see the whole town: the high school in the foreground, Hansi's Hardware on Main Street, the hospital in the distance, the mine road snaking off into the Shield. None of it gave me any pleasure.

It was cold up there. I saw that my hands were trembling, but I felt nothing. I was numb both inside and out. Though I wanted to scream with rage, to beat Ralph in the face, to fly to the ends of the earth rather than confront my dilemma, I could muster no more than the younger brother's disclaiming shrug of the shoulders.

Seventeen

Much later, over a cup of tea, Mother told me that Myrtle Dobson had thrown a scare into her. It wasn't just the way she looked, her stained teeth, her paper-thin skin. No, it wasn't only physical degeneration. Because worse for Mother was the collapse of Myrtle's will, the way everything about her denoted resignation. As she spoke Myrtle's voice ebbed into incoherence. She didn't finish thoughts, but it didn't matter to her. She merely bunched the pillows under her head and sighed, and this expressed more eloquently than words the extent of her defeat. She was prepared to take whatever blows were dealt her, whatever was coming.

This terrified Mother. When Myrtle Dobson looked dully at her wasted hands Mother wanted to scream *Don't give up!* When Myrtle sighed, "I'm going the other way," Mother's stomach turned. She wanted to catch Myrtle to her bosom, she wanted to slap her face and bring her to her senses — she didn't know which. It was an article of faith with her that no matter how bad things got life was too precious to give up on. It was something she'd learned at the funerals of the nieces and nephews who'd thrown their lives away. Maybe things didn't work out the way we planned, but life was good. It was worth going on with.

Here's what I mean. Every morning she made a point of standing at the kitchen window for five minutes. The house stood on a hill and overlooked the Pickerel River — sparkling water, trees, colorful plants growing along the riverbanks. Even in winter the sky was a dazzling blue. "The heart dances," Mother said aloud as she stood at the window. It was a romantic sentiment full of hope and belief, outrageously so, and though Mother blushed saying it, she repeated it to us and made us look out the window, too. I saw ravens there as well as hummingbirds, and impenetrable muskeg underbrush behind the sparkling waters, but I understood what Mother felt and why she wanted us to share her faith in life.

Only once had this faith been shaken — when she was in the hospital having Ralph. When the pain got so intense, she told me, she'd bit through her lower lip. She wanted to give up, and that scared her. If she was capable of one doubt, she was capable of more — perhaps the ultimate doubt, Ralph's doubt. So when she saw defeat in Myrtle Dobson, Mother imagined she might succumb to despair, too. She saw how easily the human spirit could be defeated.

She sat in the kitchen to brood about this one night. She brewed a pot of Gunpowder, putting an extra spoon of leaves in. In the living room Father opened a fresh bottle of whiskey.

"I talked to that woman again. Myrtle Dobson."

"Is that the Dobson lives along the highway?"

"Such a sad case."

"I never remember that Dobson's name. Likes netting smelts when they're spawning in spring."

"Her skin's so thin you can look through it to the bones. See blood pumping in her veins. It makes my flesh crawl."

Father stood in the doorway. "For me it's the hands. When she grips the bedsheet I think of claws, I think she's trying to scramble back from the grave."

"That's awful, Hansi." Mother chewed her lower lip. "You think Ellen looks like that to other people — people who don't know her?"

"Looks are not the issue." Father sat beside Mother. "The issue is this. Myrtle Dobson scares me because she's resigned to her fate."

"You think so?"

"Of course. She's given up. She's given in. Mrs. Dobson has already passed over from the living to the dead. She's taken Death to her heart."

So there it was. Mother's worst thoughts confirmed in simple phrases. Father could do that. Years earlier when they buried her brother it was the same. For days Mother had agonized over Stefan's death. If only she had spent more time with him, if only she'd visited him and brought him something to cheer him up — strawberry pie, he loved her strawberry pie. If only. If only that car hadn't come along right then. She brooded over every detail: the gravel strip beside the highway, the car going forty miles an hour, the horn blowing. Why hadn't she picked up the telephone and called that day? What was he doing out on the highway by himself at noon? Why had he stepped in front of the car? She tried to explain it to herself. It was like those picture puzzles you put together on the dining-room table, only one piece was missing, but you didn't find that out until you fretted over the thing for days.

At the height of her misery Father came home. He didn't even ask what was bothering her. He loosened his tie and rolled up the sleeves of his white shirt. He made a pot of coffee. Poured in some brandy. He sat on the sofa and held her hand. After a while he said, "He might not have done it on another day." When she studied his face to read what he was really saying, he added, "Then again he might have done it many times before this."

In those days they both drank coffee. Hansi liked his with lots of milk. Tina pretended she didn't understand him. She poured more coffee and made a production of putting in the milk and stirring the sugars. In the end it didn't help. Because the moment had to be faced. And she knew that Father was right.

"It was a look he had about him," Father explained. "You remember? You said something was bothering him? Oh, it must have been three months ago." Father went on before she could interrupt. "You thought he was upset about the hearing aid. But he was far beyond that by then. By then he'd made up his mind about the hearing aid and put it behind him. He was far beyond life by then." Father sipped from the mug and looked Mother in the eye. He wanted to be gentle with the truth, but he wanted the truth to be out. Mother was suffering too much. His Tina.

"Yes," he continued, "he'd made up his mind. You saw in Stefan's face the look of resignation which comes over the faces of people who decide not to go on. The look of death. I've seen it many times. In Europe on the faces of peasants driven from one place to another, forced to watch their homes burnt, children killed, women raped. I've seen it in the faces of animals dying beside the road, horses, goats, dogs no one can look after when they're fleeing for their lives, starved and defeated. And in the eyes of soldiers, too, on the battlefield, crying out for help with their voices but praying in their hearts for death."

Mother was weeping, and Father put his arms around her, but he went on. "A look saying I'm ready to accept whatever happens to me, even if it is only the same things again: suffering, and pain, even death. Washing one's hands of life, so to speak." Father's voice had drifted into a trance-like whisper. "I've seen it many times before, but I didn't recognize it right away in your brother because before I'd always seen it during disasters and slaughters and massacres. And this was different. An ordinary man living a peaceful life in the city."

"You make him sound so weak."

"Despair is the final weakness. Nothing can be so bad as to take your own life, eh?"

Father's great strength was the courage of his convictions. He saw into things without muddying them with doubt or anguish. He was sure he was right about Stefan and he was equally firm in his opinion of Ralph.

Mother admired his strength. But she wondered if he would be so strong if fate struck out at him. Because it was all well and good to be a pillar when you were not the one under fire. But would Hansi break down if he was the one suffering? Say, if he was dying of leukemia? Mother's magazine articles told her it was often the kind of men who were strong on the outside who cracked and went to pieces over emotional things.

She had been baking pies that night, and when the bell in the stove went off she got up from the kitchen table and removed them from the oven. She placed them on the counter to cool and then went to the mirror hanging in the front entrance. She studied her lined cheeks and the bags under her eyes. Fattiness had crept into her jowls. Everywhere she saw signs of physical decay. But more important she was studying the look in her eyes, the movement of her lips when she smiled into the glass. Looking for evidence of internal degeneration. Mother looked hard and long. Did she read in her tired face the first signs of despair?

Eighteen

The idea of sending Ralph and me to Toronto to get away from the inevitable finger-pointing and whispering we'd face on the streets of Red Rock came from Aunt Ellen. One night about a week after Ralph went into the hospital she talked on the phone to Mother for more than an hour, trying to console her. Mother held the receiver close to her mouth and wept into it silently. Though it was past my bedtime, I was sitting at the kitchen table shuffling through baseball cards: I was close to having the entire Braves lineup.

When she put the phone down Mother said, "Ellen thinks the boys should get away from here for a while."

Father was sipping whiskey across from me and flipping through a hardware buyer's catalogue. "Away from Red Rock?"

"I was telling her how cruel the kids at school are. How they chastise Dickie."

Father studied me. "Chastise," he repeated. "That so?"

I shrugged. "I don't give a hoot," I said, lying. Every morning my stomach was in knots as soon as I crested the hill and began the long descent toward Red Rock High and the sneers of Shrevey Russell and company. I picked up Warren Spahn's card and casually turned it over.

"They're monsters," Mother said. She had been digging in the freezer compartment of the refrigerator and had two Creamsicles in her hands, one of which she handed to me. "No better than animals."

"Tina," Father sighed. "They're just kids, they — "

"Ellen says if Ralph got away from here he'd forget all his problems. See things in a different light. Dickie too."

I looked up from my cards. I was unaware I had problems and was about to tell them so when Father said, "She could be right. I was scarcely older than Ralph when I set out for Europe. And what I learned in Rome and Milan, books could never teach."

"Ellen says they can stay with her and Albert. They'll keep an eye on them for us, but they'll be in a big city, a place where they can see things and forget what — all their problems."

Father looked at me again, gauging whether this was sinking in. "Would you like that?" he asked. "A chance to explore things together with your brother like you used to when you were little guys?"

I nodded because I knew he wanted me to and not because I thought a trip would work some brotherly magic between Ralph and me, bringing us closer together or some such thing. Also I was thinking how neat it would be to see Kensington Market. Would the man with the gold ring in his nose still be there?

"Maybe they'd even pick up a little culture," Mother added. Aunt Ellen was going to send magazines with details about Toronto's architecture and theaters, along with photographs of the harbor.

"Well," Father said, "a city is an education in itself." He swilled his whiskey and looked lost in thought.

"A change of scene," Mother said, "will do them both a world of good. Get Ralph back on the right track." When Father did not answer, she added, "But let's see how Ralph gets on."

Father grunted and put down his catalogue. He took out the ballpoint pen he kept clipped to his shirt pocket and found a page in the catalogue with blank spaces. He glanced toward Mother and asked, "What'll it cost?" He asked it as casually as inquiring what was for supper, but he was thinking about how he could afford it. Rumors continued to sweep through Red Rock. Each day brought the miners and the companies closer to a strike. And there were other rumors. The miners were talking about bringing in a new union, an international.

The company was threatening to close down the graveyard shift permanently. By the fall, maybe cut back even more. Whatever happened, Hansi's Hardware was in trouble. What a prolonged work stoppage would do to his business Father daren't even imagine. He'd already had one long talk with McGuire about his late mortgage payments.

Mother was thinking about Ralph. "Let's see how he feels," she went on, "after he gets home from the hospital." She bit into her Creamsicle and looked at me nervously before adding, "You don't think . . . once he gets home . . ."

In the silence following I expected Father to ask me to go outside to fetch something, anything to get me out of the house while the talk touched on what had happened in the garage, but he stood and went to the refrigerator for ice. He poured in the whiskey and revolved the tumbler slowly. "I don't know," he sighed. "Maybe we just have to take that chance."

"Even when Dr. McGuire — "

"Pah. McGuire was the one who said I had appendicitis that time, remember? And it was only indigestion. Wanted to put me in the hospital and keep me there over the weekend for observation. Over the weekend! Our busiest time. He thinks everybody's business falls over the doorstep like his."

"Not everything Dr. McGuire says is wrong. Look what he's done for Ralph." Mother left a silence, then added, "Look what he's done for Myrtle Dobson." A drop of Creamsicle fell from her lip and she spotted it off her pink angora sweater with a tissue. "I don't think I'd feel so bad if I was in her shoes and McGuire was my doctor."

Father looked at her oddly as if he heard a warning in her voice but couldn't place it. "Tina," he said, "the point is this. No matter what we do to make sure Ralph won't try the same thing again, nothing is guaranteed. He may come home and be perfectly all right for the rest of his life. Never a thought again of — of anything rash. But you know how he is. How easily he swings one way or the other. He might hang around here happy as a clam for six months after he comes out and nothing happens. Then one day just out of the blue . . ."

"You don't want to throw him out into the world too soon."

"Of course not." Father sighed. "But if he's going to do it, he's going to, and nothing we say will make a jot of difference."

"So there's nothing we can do?"

"Nothing we do will matter. Keeping him home for two weeks, two months, two years won't change anything — fundamental." He studied me to see if I agreed, and I dropped my eyes to the baseball cards laid out on the table: I'd recently made a trade for Lew Burdette but could not get Bob Hazle from anyone.

"But Dr. McGuire says — "

"And neither will McGuire's head-shrinker."

He fixed me with his eye before taking a resolute swallow of whiskey, making sure I knew just what he thought on that subject. He'd treated us to his views before. To Father, as to most people then, psychiatry was a lot of puffed-up talk that never came down to the essential issue. What mattered was whether people had the backbone to rise above the troubles the world threw at them. It was a matter of will and will-power, and if Ralph had the backbone, he'd survive no matter what awful things came his way. If he didn't, then he only got what was coming to him.

Nineteen

Toronto in the fall: throbbing crowds, the pong of hockey in the air, the jazz of autumn leaves. We'd traveled a long way from granite-bound Red Rock, and when we hopped off the train at Union Station the first thing we saw was the roof of the Royal York, gleaming copper-green in the morning sun. We stood on the curb, hands on hips, and gawked. Then we took in the rose-tinted skyscrapers rearing into the clouds, the bustle of businessmen on the sidewalks, yellow taxis honking, neon signs flashing the red, white, and blue of Coke, du Maurier, Blue Ribbon, the fug of idling motors, a policeman in the intersection blowing his whistle and waving his arms. On the sidewalk a hobo dragged a three-wheeled wagon exploding with rags and oddments of machinery. Young women smelling of flowers tripped by, their arms laden with papers. Dust, horns blatting, diesel fumes. Downtown Toronto.

When he'd taken it all in Ralph ruffled his rooster-tailing head of hair and grinned from ear to ear. He said loudly, *what the hell.* It was the invitation a kid brother hungers after. He gave me a smile at once teasing and conspiratorial. Phony, actually. A Cheshire cat smile I instantly distrusted.

Aunt Ellen was at the doctor's for cobalt treatments that morning and Uncle Albert at a convention in Montreal, so we were making our way to their place on our own. We hoisted our shabby suitcases off the curb, Ralph's with one strap missing but held together with a leather belt, and walked along York Street toward Queen. Sidewalks of rushing people. At Queen we boarded the streetcar and rattled past City Hall. The morning sun warmed us. The streetcar windows were up and we felt the breezes off the street and heard the horns of passing cars and the shouts of news-hawks. Would we never hear the end of the Russians and *Sputnik?* Trolley cars clustered at Yonge Street, clanking and clanging. We transferred, heading north toward Rosedale, where Aunt Ellen lived.

We had no idea what we were doing. I sat on the edge of the seat and held my suitcase close. I watched Ralph's face, tense with excitement. News-hawks, taxicabs. Where was Maple Leaf Gardens, the Royal Ontario Museum, the univer-sity? His blue eyes darted up and down the trolley car and surveyed the street where women in crinolines paraded by and men in dark suits hustled along with their briefcases and umbrellas. Some things caught us off guard: blacks in busi-ness suits, clusters of Orientals, two women at the rear of the bus chattering in a foreign tongue — Italian? At College Street Ralph signaled to me and we jumped off and walked toward the treed patch of city to the north. Queen's Park.

It took my breath away. Lush green lawns, stone foot-paths, flower beds — some in designs of flags. In the distance red brick buildings covered in ivy. The university. Men and women sauntered past hand in hand or bustled by to classes. Briefcases, books, satchels, umbrellas. It was fall. The maples and oaks were losing their leaves — but what colors! Black squirrels the size of tomcats hopped about gathering stuff for winter.

We bought sandwiches in waxed paper at a stand and sat on the grass to eat. Ralph took one bite from his and passed the rest to me. He lay back and sighed.

"You know," he said, "the sky is higher here. Pli alta. In Red Rock the clouds get right on my chest. They choke me." He placed his hands round his throat and gagged for effect. Since his return from hospital he'd taken to falling silent suddenly and staring vacantly for minutes at a time, feigning self-control.

But he wasn't fooling me. I'd been watching him care-fully out of the corners of my eyes. Yes, watching him with the devotion I would always feel for him, but now too with apprehension. For he'd lost that nervous drive that made him hurl things in the air and tear his hair. Or suppressed it. In its place he affected calm. He was taking things just as they came, it said. Disinterested. His eyes, which were bright indigo when he went to the hospital, had faded now to lusterless blue. In anyone the change would have been upsetting, but in Ralph it was uncanny. I'd seen the eyes of zombies on "Late Night Chiller," and Ralph's were vacant like that. Spooky. I anticipated any moment the outbursts of violence he was famous for, I was steeled for them, but they never came. What he offered instead was an engaging but phony smile.

Here was the puzzling thing: I had the feeling he was waiting for me to do something. Me, the devoted younger brother who had always followed. First with sandpails round the yard when we were toddlers. Later learning Meccano from him and Tinkertoys and how to line up the plastic soldiers from cereal boxes. I trailed him to school when he carried *Dick and Jane* and I was still wearing knee pants. Then to the sandlot ball games where he put me in the field while he and his buddies got to pitch and take turns batting. "Dickie," he'd shout, "go fetch the ball," and I would recklessly retrieve it from Mrs. Valencourt's garden, trampling her peonies in kid brother innocence while Mrs. V. raged behind her chintz curtains. Always I had followed, but now I sensed he was waiting for me to lead. What did he expect me to do?

Maybe something to acknowledge what he'd whispered to me in the hospital. He'd never said anything like it again. When Father brought him home from Red Rock General I was in terror. I avoided his eyes but waited for him to corner me and swear me to secrecy. I half expected him to force me to prick my wrist with a sewing needle and make a blood compact.

So I lurked around doorways and fled the empty house. At nights I left him alone in his room and sat with Father at the bottom of the yard listening to the Braves march toward the pennant on the radio. As the days passed and he said nothing I studied his eyes in moments when he was unguarded — at the dinner table, or listening to one of Father's anecdotes. Nothing there. No hint he was only biding his time, waiting to spring something on me.

First I rejoiced, thinking he'd given the whole thing up. Then I distrusted my memory. Maybe I had imagined it, the way I imagined conversations between my parents when I tried to understand their motives and actions. For days I was convinced he no longer remembered what he'd said: that drugged and dazed as he was, he'd lost his memory. Finally I thought, he won't hold me to it, he's forgotten everything. By the time we were lounging in Queen's Park I was feeling pretty cocky.

I was sketching some of the stone buildings in my notebook, shading with lead pencil the snaking line of mortised joints up the walls to the blue sky, trying to capture the unusual shimmering light that limestone reflects at midday.

"What I like about Toronto," Ralph said, "is everyone here is in it for themselves. You see?"

I nodded absently.

"They're so obvious about it too. About their naked desire." He was toying with a stick, a foot-long piece of broken tree branch, and suddenly he threw it at a passing cab — *whack* it went against the metal door. He laughed when the cabbie gave us the finger.

He fixed me with that brown-spotted eye and repeated, "Naked, Dickie." He nodded toward the sidewalk where a businessman was hurrying by. "Look at that three-piece suit strutting past, he's out to make it and the devil take the hindmost." He waited for this to sink in. He was wearing a white T-shirt and tugged at the sleeves, straightening it. "Because there's so much to be gained, and this is a paltry businessman, someone with bonds to sell, or whatever. Don't you see it, Dickie, don't you understand the simple miners' philosophy of snatch and grab?"

As usual I didn't, but more important than what I saw was what I wanted to see — the old Ralph back again, for one. I asked him, "You trying to tell me something?"

He laughed, snorted, really. "Only that I'm in love with

what I see. Kun birdoj, kun bestoj, kun floroj. Look around, Dickie, Toronto in its golden apple prime. Trees aflame, the sky a canvas of hues. Nature in its carnal dance. La danco volupta. Hear the throb of commerce and the stir of our fellow man."

He stood abruptly and shook his fist in the air. "Shit," he said, "love's not it at all. Take is what it's all about. Take whatever you want and the hell with everyone else. That's what it's all about, Dickie. Don't let anyone ever tell you different."

He said it with such forced conviction I thought for a moment I was hearing Patsy Johnson gushing over Wordsworth's daffodils in English class. And then I caught on: it was all just hurt and anger pretending to be something else. My heart sank. I realized how foolish I'd been to imagine he was waiting for some sign from me. He was not waiting for me, he was not waiting for anyone in God's unholy creation. He was only waiting for the right moment to bring it to an end.

Twenty

We spent a long evening at Aunt Ellen's flipping through photo albums and learning about Uncle Albert's latest triumph, a share in a race horse owned by E. P. Taylor. Aunt Ellen questioned us about Mother's health and then took us out to the garage where we found two tennis racquets and a can of balls. The next morning, she said, she'd take us to the Rosedale Tennis Club and arrange lessons. Though we tried to look keen, we were not enthusiastic until she added, "And your uncle Albert's left you twenty dollars each for a night on the town."

That was more what we had in mind.

So we trudged the several blocks to the tennis courts the next morning and swung at balls under the hot sun and praised the tomato sandwiches Aunt Ellen had fixed for our lunch. But our thoughts raced ahead to Yonge Street where there were bars and clubs and dancing girls.

We slicked back our hair and put on white shirts, leaving the top two buttons open, the way James Dean did. The streetcar dropped us off at Bloor and Avenue Road, so the first thing we saw getting down was the Park Plaza Hotel. Ralph elbowed me in the ribs and we took the elevator to the Roof Garden and the patio bar overlooking the city. I slipped past the bartender while Ralph ordered a beer, and we stood outside, peering over the patio wall at the city. He pointed out the Conservatory of Music and Varsity Stadium. I looked down Bloor apprehensively. (Yes, I'm afraid of heights, I gripped the stone balustrade with white knuckles.) My stomach fluttered. It seemed a long drop to the sidewalk, though Ralph assured me it was less than a hundred feet. He swept his arm from one building to another. Behind the red brick Conservatory we picked out the ivy-draped spires of Wycliffe College. Through the rainbow of maples, the long tiled roof of Hart House. I studied the pitch of the roof and the mottled stone walls. Far in the distance shimmered the Engineering buildings, which Ralph wanted to visit.

When he'd sipped a little, Ralph gave me the rest of his beer to finish and wandered off toward the bar. I stood with my back resting against the stone wall and looked at the other drinkers. A young couple whispered and giggled at a table in the corner. Men in business suits studied papers laid out on the table before them. Two men closer talked about baseball. Henry Aaron was on a home run streak and Warren Spahn going for a twenty-win season. I felt a special affection for Warren Spahn because he was left-handed like me. Also chunky. Ball players, I'd noticed, especially pitchers, did not have to be sleek, svelte athletes. Even the great Babe was overweight.

When I finished drinking the beer I felt quite bold, so I sauntered across the patio toward the bar. Ralph was leaning against it, chatting with the bartender. They laughed suddenly and the bartender gave me the eye. Ralph placed some money on the bar, then he walked over to me, extending his arm in a brotherly embrace. "It's time for Yonge Street," he said and winked back at the bartender.

We stood at the stone wall for one last look at the city lights, studying the traffic and bustle of Bloor. The sounds of car horns and trolleys competed with the cries of gulls careering round us. One perched on a ledge and sat opening and closing its beak, breathing hard. Suddenly it plunged down. We watched it dive toward the street and I held my breath, waiting for it to swoop upward just above the concrete. Ralph said, "Now there's a trick worth learning." He slapped me on the back and added, "But what we want is Lola and the Damselles of Denmark."

First there was dinner at a little Italian place around the corner where Ralph ordered more beer and poured some in my glass when the waiter wasn't looking. Plates of pasta and a salad with black olives and feta cheese. And after dinner Ralph bought some cigars. He rolled one between his fingers and wet it with his lips before lighting up.

Along Bloor to Yonge, and south past the book shops and shoe stores and cinemas. The sidewalk was crowded with couples walking arm in arm and packs of single men in baggies and polished loafers. Cars overflowing with teenagers, engines revving at intersections, the bright glint of metal, and then the squealing tires. In front of a place called Deuces Wild a black man with a boater and cane winked and tipped his head toward a stairway covered with posters of Rosa and Rita, the Solsolita Sisters. Across Dundas a man was selling popcorn and peanuts from a pushcart: crippled in both legs, he wore the decorations of a war veteran on the breast of his frayed jacket. Ralph knocked cigar ash into the curb and tossed the vet a silver dollar.

Lola and the Dancing Damselles were at the Honeycomb: "Direct from Paris — Exotic Entertainment." Ralph pushed on the saloon doors and we swam into the submarine glow of a smoky joint with a bar at one end and a stage at the other. A man in a white dinner jacket looked at us suspiciously for a moment, then shrugged and ushered us to a table. It was right up front. When our beers came the waiter set them on the edge of the stage where the strippers danced.

I looked around: at the bar stocked with bottles high as the ceiling, at the other men sitting in shadows, dim silhouettes raising glasses to mouths, at the stage where any moment Lola would do her numbers. At Ralph, aglow with triumph and affected calm. The smart sophisticate. He unwrapped a cigar and winked at me. The blue flare of his match threw ghostly shadows around his eye sockets. He flicked the match to the floor.

I felt pretty sharp myself. I raised my glass of beer and basked in the heady aromas of hops and malt and debauchery. We'd come a long way from Red Rock, and the distance we'd traveled could be tasted in that beer. Then the stage lights went down.

The Dancing Damselles came out first, six slinky girls

wearing black net stockings and short skirts, bows in their hair done up to resemble rabbits' ears. They looked younger than in the marquee photos. At one end of the line was a blonde with short hair and high, firm breasts. She cupped them self-consciously before the music began and looked awkwardly into the audience with round eyes. My tongue stuck in my throat. I shifted on my chair.

Halfway through their second number the Damselles were joined by Lola, in an identical costume but crimson where the Damselles' were pink. A ripple of applause. Lola removed the bow from her waist and threw it into the crowd. Whoops of approval. The Damselles swayed in rhythm behind her, clapping as Lola tossed off her rabbit ears, her lamé slippers, one black stocking and then the other. The men were getting excited. Chanting her name: Lo-la, Lo-la. She produced a yellow see-through scarf and drew it between her fingers, teasing as she danced. The men cheered and clapped. Called out Lola's name. She flaunted the scarf between her long legs as she strutted about the stage, half a foot of silky yellow projecting between her fingers.

Then she spotted me. She came to the edge of the stage and leaned over us. Her breasts were powdery and pink. She was a redhead with thick pouting lips. "Know what this is, big fella?" She rolled her eyes at me and then mugged for the crowd. A titter ran around the room. My ridiculous ears went red, they were neon signs advertising to everyone in the bar that I'd never been laid. Lola said mockingly, "Uh-huh." There was a burst of laughter near the bar. But Lola wasn't laughing. She arched her back, thrust both hands between her legs and drew the scarf up through her crotch, jerking the last few inches in short spasms. Some men stood and cheered. Lola dropped to her knees with her head thrown back and ran her tongue around her lips. After the cheering stopped she stood, spun the scarf over her head, and dropped it into the palm of one of the Dancing Damselles.

When Lola had stripped completely she bowed, gave the crowd a big wink, and disappeared. The stage lights went off. And when they came back on, Lola's yellow scarf was on the table in front of me but Ralph had disappeared. I gawked around, thinking he'd gone to the bar for something, and a man behind me rolled his eyes toward the ceiling and smiled knowingly. It took me several minutes to understand why and then I felt my ears go red again and turned my eyes back to my glass of beer where I riveted them until Ralph returned in half an hour.

"Long time no see," he said, affecting a casual air. And then, "We need more cold drinks here." He lit up another cigar, leaned back in his chair, and blew smoke rings over our heads, a jagged smile curling his lips.

After the waiter put our beers on the table Ralph leaned across and whispered, "Beleta knabino, Dickie, beleta." And I knew if I wanted to I could go upstairs, too.

I sat there a long time thinking about that.

Twenty-one

Two things made sitting in that bar terrible. One, I knew if I didn't walk up the stairs as Ralph had he would tease me until it drove me crazy. Though at fifteen I was just a kid who'd never as much as kissed a girl. And more important, I'd fallen in love with the short-haired blonde at the end of the dancing line: I wanted to confess my love to her so much my head hurt. Ralph thought this was laughable. He had told me all about the miners' philosophy of love-em-and-leave-em, about wham-bam-thank-you-ma'am, but I didn't want a sleazy twenty minutes with the pretty blonde, I wanted starlit walks, I wanted hand-holding, I wanted tender kisses under the moon. So I sat there nursing my beer, feeling Ralph's eyes on me, and condemned myself to endless jokes about not getting it up.

Not that I wasn't watching him, too. When he'd leaned over the patio at the Park Plaza and peered down Bloor I'd tensed with fear. Imagined, looking down, the mess of blood and clothes he would make if he leapt. I looked for a certain flicker in his eyes, and the way he roostered back his straw hair. But I'd seen nothing.

Of course I was a fool to believe I could figure out just by watching him what he was feeling.

Where would he try it? I asked myself, knowing one moment of letting down my guard was all it would take. One moment too many spent mooning over the blonde in the chorus line. Yes, I knew it was only a matter of time, it was clear in the ironic smile he'd flashed me in Queen's Park, a smile challenging me to beat him just once at a game he'd invented.

What could I do?

First I calculated on his flair for the dramatic. Having failed once, Ralph would not settle for anything less than spectacular. When he'd pointed out the sights around the Park Plaza, I watched his eyes calculating the distance from the patio to the sidewalk. Would he jump? I was ready to haul him back. That morning at Aunt Ellen's I'd stood beside him in the bathroom while he shaved — and checked when he bathed. Was he a slasher? I hated blood, but I stashed towels under the bed to stanch it. I'd guarded my trouser belt, too.

I anticipated every strategy he could devise against himself, hoping to intercept it. In my sketchbook I made a list of things to avoid:

tall buildings
razor blades
pills/potions
cars, buses
guns

But I soon saw it would never do. The opportunities to kill yourself were legion. A man had too much access to himself for someone else to stop him. Murder was easier to prevent than suicide.

The morning after our night on the town Aunt Ellen suggested a trip to High Park. "A good idea," Ralph whispered to me when she stepped out of the room. "Clear our heads." He added, "Anyway, I'm sick of watching you behave like a lovesick pup. That glazed look in your eyes." He laughed, but I detected a flicker in his eyes and concluded something was up.

When we stood for the trolley car I recalled newspaper items about people throwing themselves in front of trains, and when I glanced at Ralph's feet they seemed to be inching toward the tracks. So before the train rumbled to a stop I tugged him backward, feigning fear.

At the park he headed straight for the swinging bridge, where I stood beside him and kept up a steady stream of engineering questions — force, stress — all calculated to engage his mechanistic mind as we eyed the water swirling twenty feet below. The eddying water made an inviting vortex, you wanted to jump. We placed our hands on the rope handrail and Ralph's fingers clenched and unclenched around it as we talked.

We ate lunch at a counter and throughout the meal he smiled at me, not the open smile of our boyhood days but a measured grin, a smirk saying, all right, I see what you're up to, Jack.

Yes, that's what it was, a look of recognition, and for a moment there in the park I felt quite smug. I suppose I expected him to say "You win." Something like that. An acknowledgment. I'd convinced myself I was very clever, reading his intentions, anticipating disasters.

Instead he smiled that bitten way and offered me a cigar, which I refused in favor of another plate of fries. "I appreciate it," he said. And when I feigned ignorance, he added, "Your little schemes to keep me from doing myself in." He held up his hand to stop me from interrupting. "I really do. But you needn't bother." Blue smoke scarved his face, lending an ashen pallor to his cheeks. "Save your energy for a girl."

"What?" I was shaking salt onto french fries.

"La knabino. Forget trying to keep me from myself."

"You know what your biggest mistake is?"

"I have a feeling I'm going to find out."

"Thinking you know everything about me."

He grunted and blew smoke rings. "Dickie . . ."

"How I feel about you, about Dad . . ." I was poised to make an impressive speech, a speech invoking loyalty and sacrifice and things like that. Brotherly love.

He laughed at me. "You're a riot, Dickie, just listen to the way you talk sometimes, but not even you can believe that romantic nonsense about family and the old Frudel fortitude."

When he saw I wouldn't deny it, he went on. "Anyway, they told me about the famous trust." He looked away and roostered his hair.

"And?"

"It's worth a shot, eh? Just to show them."

"Right. You can't keep the Frudels down."

He sat considering that for a few moments while I stuffed french fries into my face.

"Just imagine," he said. He took a drag of his cigar. "California. Oranges. Multe de beleta knabinoj." He shaped a Coke bottle outline with his hands.

"That Dad, he — "

"In California, they say, there's two girls for every guy."

I lurched to my feet, spilling french fries onto the floor, alarming the other diners at the counter, and threw both arms around him. It was a gesture worthy of Ralph at his impulsive best. My bearish hug took him by surprise. Hot ash sprinkled on his wrist. He jerked his arm away.

"Oh lord," I said, "oh lordy-o."

He smiled. Not the smile of calculation he'd been affecting throughout the trip, not even the smirk of superiority he turned on his enemies, but the crazy smile of our boyhood when he leapt from behind doors terrifying Mother or peed in Mrs. Valencourt's flower bed. An ear-to-ear smile. My heart jumped in my chest. My first thought was Ralph would go to California after all and realize his dreams.

Then I thought (living up to my reputation as romantic fool) it might even be better we'd experienced the bad times. I saw it as a test we'd come through with flying colors. Now we'd all understand and love each other better — Mother, Father, Ralph, and me. We'd appreciate the family. Like the broken branch of the proverb, we'd bent but hadn't broken and would be stronger for having suffered the ordeal.

I felt warm inside and my hands trembled. I'd forgotten the girl, how I imagined the silk of blond hair would feel on my belly, her high, firm breasts. I'd forgotten High Park, Centre Island, Maple Leaf Gardens, the stone buildings of the university. I'd forgotten Ralph's black moods and his cruelty, too. Erased from memory. I wanted only to go home and say to Mother and Father, here is my brother back who once was lost. Ralph Bascom Frudel, wunderkind, dreamer, lover of life.

I clutched him to my bosom, my crazy, my improvident brother.

Twenty-two

Hansi's Hardware went bad fast. One day it was orders for bags of cement, pallets of shingles, gallons of paint, and the next it was an empty store on Saturday morning, not one miner buying pickerel rigs. Hansi's footfall echoed round the walls. One day it was four-figure cheques from the Safeway and the next it was McGuire calling him in for a little chat. In no time at all Hansi went from prosperous burgher to prostrate bankrupt.

He might have seen it coming with the devaluation of the dollar. He bought the *Free Press* every evening and studied the business pages. First the drop in the dollar's value was called a return to a fair market price: it had fallen from a high of $1.08 U.S. to even par. That was okay with him; he believed in fair market value. When it dropped to $.95 U.S. the papers called it a temporary adjustment. He felt uneasy. He remembered the federal income tax was brought in after the war as a temporary measure. Politicians had a way of saying one thing and meaning something else; of doing something entirely different. He'd learned that in the war when Churchill and Roosevelt first denounced Stalin and then embraced him. But no one expected what they actually got, the sub–ninety cent dollar: the Diefendollar.

Things didn't look good. Despite the Pentagon's zeal over the space program, despite the President's speeches welcoming new states to the Union, the realization of Manifest Destiny, despite the expansion of AT&T and the ribbon cuttings at the new aerospace plants springing up around the country, despite record profits at United States Steel, despite the silliness of Hula Hoops and the frenzy of "Jailhouse Rock," prospects for the future looked bad. Hansi should have seen the end coming with the rumblings from Cuba.

He should have seen that Red Rock was doomed when rumors about conveyor belts started again. Gerry Stockton reported, "They're bringing them over from Cleveland on flatcars."

"I told you," replied Hansi. They were leaning on the counter in the hardware store. "The company won't stand around waiting for the union to shit or get off the pot."

"Those belts are nearly three miles long." Gerry had come in to commiserate with Hansi. He jabbed his cigarette in the air. "And it takes four of them to set up for production." Gerry smoked more now the rumors Red Rock was on the downturn were becoming reality.

"Didn't I tell you?" Hansi slapped the counter. He sometimes felt like smoking a cigarette himself. "Didn't I say the miners would price themselves out of work?"

"All those wildcats and slowdowns."

"They say it's the company." Hopeless Mike stood at the back of the store. "They say it's the company wants bigger profits."

"Who says?"

"Down at the Hall at Saturday's meeting — "

"Pah," said Hansi. "The union's responsible for these conveyors in the first place. The owners wouldn't have bothered hauling those belts halfway across the continent if the union hadn't forced their hand. Can you imagine the cost of transporting those things?"

Hopeless Mike said, "What about the company threatening to pack up and move to Algoma?" He sidled up between Gerry and Hansi and looked from one to the other. "That's industrial blackmail."

"The union calls it blackmail because the union has to find a way of saving face." While he talked, Hansi fingered his neck where a boil was threatening to erupt. Nerves, Dr. McGuire said, were responsible for them — nerves and whiskey. "The company's just doing what's good business."

"Maximizing profits," Gerry chimed in.

"Exactly. But the union got the men in this mess by lying about company profits and how the working man was being cheated. Feeding them dreams about high wages. And now the whole thing's blown up in their faces the union's looking for someone to blame."

"You can bet it won't be the union."

Hopeless Mike said, "The union's done a lot of good for the men." He took one of Gerry's cigarettes and struck a match. "Good wages aren't the only thing. A hospital plan."

"Also the union's responsible for the bad things you see around Red Rock. For the wildcats setting people against each other. For the fellas losing their jobs. For this — " Hansi swung his arm round the empty store. "And God knows what all else."

Gerry nodded. "For the Germans backing out of contracts." He lit one cigarette off another. "Because every time they tool up for production over there we delay over here while the miners strike and we dicker over $4.35 an hour or $4.52."

Hansi said, "There's your union for you, Mike." He undid the buttons on his shirt cuffs and pushed up the sleeves past his elbows. "There's what's responsible for all of us facing bankruptcy in this godforsaken hole of a town. There's your greed."

The three men fell silent and like birds swifting a branch stepped outside as one. They could hear the rumble of blasting from the mines. It was drizzling. Each water droplet seemed to contain a seed of iron dust. When Hansi rubbed his forearm the water smeared red on his skin. He sighed.

And at home he said to Tina, "That bloody McGuire called me again today." They sat at the kitchen table watching the hands of the clock slide past midnight. Tina'd put on her housecoat at ten and Hansi had soaked in a hot bath while he read the evening paper, but neither wanted to go to bed. They knew what torture waited there, hours of tossing and sighing. At best, they could hope for a little drowsiness just before sunrise.

"Ellen phoned today."

"Here," Hansi said. He reached across the table and splashed whiskey into Tina's tea. There was a time when she would have put her hand over the mouth of the cup.

"The boys are having a swell time."

"That's good. We did a good thing there."

"But with Ellen it won't be long now, I think."

"Don't take it on yourself," said Hansi. He reached and touched Tina's cheek. She hadn't recovered her looks after Ralph had gone into hospital. Dark pouches spread from her eyes to the corners of her mouth. She knit her fingers constantly.

"Can we afford it? Another trip to Toronto, I mean. Because I can stay with Ellen when I get there."

Hansi sighed. "It doesn't matter now. As well in the pockets of the CPR as the Toronto-Dominion." He poured more whiskey.

He and Tina were accustomed to long pauses in their conversations.

"How did it happen so fast?" he wondered aloud.

"It was the cobalt," Tina said. "They thought it would send the tumors into remission, but it did the opposite. Speeded everything up. Sometimes, they say, it works that way. There's no predicting." She sipped at her drink. "And now they say she should have gone to Rochester where they have those blood machines and even though it's terribly expensive Albert would've paid because what's expense to him, but they found out too late."

Hansi stared at Tina. He thought, we're carrying on two different conversations. Have things really got so bad?

"Don't," Tina said. Her hand was on Hansi's wrist. "Don't pick."

Hansi studied his nails, stained blood red. "I didn't realize." He fingered a boil on his neck.

She poured more tea and splashed in whiskey. "And will McGuire take everything? The house? Everything?"

"Whatever's in my name, the lawyer says. The house, the car. The bank accounts. I should have put them in your name long ago."

"But not the trust."

"There's no way the bloodsuckers will touch that trust."

"At least there's that."

"There's enough for Ralph's tuition. Two years, anyway. And after that . . ." Hansi stared out the kitchen window. In the distance the lights from the night shift working the open pits glowed yellow tinged red by iron dust. An owl hooted in the yard. "And a few thousand to get us on our feet. Buy another hot dog stand, maybe. Or start up again in real estate. I was good at that." He looked at Tina. "It isn't so bad, you know. I'm still not an old man, and I've always been able to turn a profit at something. And I've got my health."

"Yes." Tina's voice was choked with tears. "You do."

"As long as nothing else happens."

"Yes. As long as nothing else . . ."

"Well, how much bad luck does one family get?"

Twenty-three

Every morning when Tina woke she felt she was choking to death. Something was blocking her windpipe, something small and sharp and very painful — a chicken bone, maybe. She sat up in bed, being careful not to wake Hansi, who rasped in a drunken stupor but woke with a start at the slightest disturbance.

Tina crept into the bathroom. She stood before the mirror. What she saw there was not comforting. She steeled herself before running a glass of cold water, and she swallowed it quickly to take the edge off the pain she felt in her gullet. Then a projectile of vomit spewed out her mouth. This had been going on for months. Tina had lost twelve pounds. She was losing patience with her body. She was beginning to fear she would also lose control of her mind.

She asked herself, could I have swallowed a chicken bone? She stood before the mirror with her tongue out and peered down her throat. Her tonsils looked back at her, they jiggled when she breathed. Otherwise she saw nothing.

For a month she'd been going to bed imagining she'd choke to death in her sleep. She lay sweating on the sheets, expecting any moment to be her last. One morning she reasoned with herself as she studied the ceiling: a bone lodged in her throat would either have choked her already or passed through to her stomach and been digested. So it had to be something else. Perhaps it was a tumor. She poked around her throat but felt nothing out of the ordinary — sinews, muscles, neck bones.

Finally she decided it was a sign. Her body was insisting she tell Hansi about the leukemia.

It was not something she wanted to do. He was already fretting about cash flow and mortgages. He didn't need another thing to worry about. So she said to herself, I will speak to him after I visit the doctor.

She kept a notebook where she recorded her symptoms: headache, sore back, vomiting. The notebook was filling up. There were patterns: when the headaches started behind her ears, her back ached; when they started in her temples she vomited. Secretively Tina tracked the progress of her illness. And she checked herself frequently in the mirror, looking for something in the eyes, because it was in the eyes she'd seen the death of Ellen. And Myrtle Dobson.

One night over dinner she asked Hansi, "Do my eyes look odd? Inflamed?" She'd rehearsed the speech carefully, pretending she was only concerned about a speck of dust that had blown in her eye while she was sweeping the driveway. At a second's notice she was prepared to shrug and take up another subject.

That seemed like a long time ago, before the episode at the school even, when she was waiting for the results from the doctor. That's when she was still thinking no use troubling Hansi, it's probably nothing. Anyway, he was preoccupied with interest rates and schemes for refinancing. With a bottle at his elbow and a tumbler of whiskey nearby, he fretted away the evenings while Tina flipped through magazines and brooded about pains in her body. He was often up past midnight and came to bed without her noticing.

So she worried in solitude. She spent most afternoons sipping chamomile tea and staring blankly at the walls while the CBC spluttered away in the background: John Drainie, The Happy Gang. Often she read — or reread — the letters she received from Ellen.

These letters alarmed her. Tumorigenic this, Ellen wrote in a schoolgirl's hand, carcinogenic that. Unpronounceable clinical words meaning nausea, blood, pain. And then leaping off the page, "They strapped me down for the incisions." Tina swore she would never feel envy or anger about Ellen again. She had been a fool to resent Ellen's superior airs. She should have laughed them off. She should have changed subjects whenever Ellen's boasting started to irritate her.

After her preliminary results came back Tina said, I'll wait until the weekend because one day will not make any difference and on the weekend Hansi won't be preoccupied and we can discuss it calmly. She rehearsed that scene, too, husband and wife sitting at the table over a pot of something strong but not bitter — Queen Mary — talking the whole thing through dispassionately. There were entire conversations in her head, words spoken first with calm indifference, then restrained emotion, and finally warm compassion. Because at first Hansi wouldn't understand why she'd kept it from him, and then he'd be sorry for being angry and he would take her in his arms and tell her everything would be all right. She'd tell him about the experiments with cobalt and the blood machines in Rochester, the miracle treatments, and he would pat her hand and tell her everything would be all right.

That was two weeks before Ralph drank the orange juice and then went into the garage, and in a way Tina was relieved she hadn't worked up the courage to tell Hansi before that happened. He was already a nervous wreck. Boils had broken out all over his neck and back. He sat up every night with a bottle of whiskey. He slept fitfully. He could talk of nothing but layoffs, conveyor belts, pit closures, and mortgage payments. There were pads of lined paper in a kitchen drawer with figures scratched on them.

But the first time she saw Myrtle Dobson at Red Rock General, Tina went weak inside. Myrtle was the picture of Tina's worst fantasies: shrunken frame, glassy eyes, gray skin. She had a tuft of hair sticking up on her forehead, reminding Tina of a diseased mouse. Emaciated, Tina said to herself. And worse still, Myrtle had lost her will to live. When Tina looked at Myrtle she saw herself and she said, how can I do this to Hansi?

Then after the tests came back she said, how can I not tell him?

To Dr. McGuire she said, "It's a bad time for us."

117

And Dr. McGuire said, "Tina, it's never not a bad time, and you can't afford to wait. We have to catch this right away. We have to hope for remissions. Possibly a cure. You simply cannot afford to wait."

Surprisingly she felt little pain. In the week after seeing Dr. McGuire she woke each morning expecting cramps in her stomach, or paralyzing headaches. She poked the flesh around her organs trying to find a sensitive spot. She felt nothing. Only sometimes in the afternoon she felt tired and wanted a pot of strong tea to revive herself. Sometimes her eyes seemed weaker as the day wore on. Maybe she needed glasses. Maybe nothing's really wrong, she thought, remembering what Hansi said about Red Rock's doctors. Quacks, he called them. And worse.

But Dr. McGuire said, "It's not the kind of thing where you get symptoms like swelling and pains. It's in the blood. You've had it awhile now. And you're running out of time."

So finally Tina decided, as soon as the boys go to Toronto I'll tell him. That will be the best anyway, because with them out of the house we can talk without being disturbed.

She remembered the intimacy of their talks when they were first married, lying together in bed and whispering plans into the dark. She'd rested her head on Hansi's chest and thrown one knee across his legs, listening to his heart lug-dubbing in her ear. Tina felt good about that. She made sure there was lots of Queen Mary on hand. And checked Hansi's whiskey cabinet. She rehearsed how she'd start the conversation. "Hansi," she'd say, "you remember how Ellen looked when she visited last time?"

Myrtle Dobson's death made her more determined. After an hour of weeping Tina said to herself, at least for Myrtle the pain is over, and at least now her family can get on with their lives. She pictured Myrtle's six kids in a circle round their bewildered father: his business was doing as badly as Hansi's, and now he had lost his wife.

Then Tina said, I cannot put it off any longer. She knew whatever Hansi said, whatever pain she brought him, it would be less than if she kept silent. It wasn't fair not to tell him. She bought a yellow dress and had her hair done up. The cold wave was popular that year. She stood before the mirror and did her best to mask the pouches under her eyes with cosmetics. There was no question the disease was moving in.

Tina got down on her knees at the foot of her bed and prayed.

Twenty-four

I was angry. After that brief moment of intimacy at the lunch counter in High Park Ralph had shut me out. We'd hugged each other and looked into each other's eyes: In his I saw the brown spot, but no fear; I hoped he saw in mine the old Frudel fortitude.

We pushed aside our food and lit up fresh cigars and sat puffing and studying the ends of our smokes like backroom boys. I trembled with anticipation. I expected Ralph to lean closer and speak to me from the depths of his heart. Ordinarily he was not an easy person to talk to: he put up walls, he protected himself. But from time to time he let down the walls and told me his innermost feelings. This time was different. He smiled, and he paid minute attention to relighting and inhaling his Perfecto, but he said no more about why he went to the garage that night or how he felt about the trust or anything that meant anything to him at all.

So we sat in silence.

I did not make the mistake of thinking he was waiting to be drawn out. That was not his style. No. Ralph was intense, manic, demanding, pushy, fierce, and arrogant, but he was not passive. When he wanted to, he forced his opinions and feelings on you — once confessing he'd pushed a classmate down a stairway and stolen his comic books, and the night he lost his virginity treating me to every detail, including what he'd done with the condom afterward. Ralph was forever prattling and emoting. But between us conversation was at his initiative.

And as the younger brother I was cast in the role of silent partner, of secret sharer: Sancho Panza to his Don Quixote.

So when Ralph turned his cup bottom-side-up and pushed his sandwich plate to the middle of the table, I knew our talk in the diner was over. I put my fork down with a sigh and gritted my teeth. I knew there was nothing to be done about it. We paid our bill and left a tip.

We went for one last look at the pond.

The water sparkled in the sunlight. I had my camera along and I took a photo of Ralph against the backdrop of the pond and the sky — cigar in one hand, sporting a white T-shirt. (I still have that photo somewhere, and one he took of me, an ungainly teenager with big hands, looking like someone trying very hard to understand what was happening to him.)

Swans paddled along the water's edge, feeding. Two swam up to us, cocking their heads, studying us out of big black eyes. The nearer spread his wings and flapped them on the water, spraying droplets onto our shoes.

"Gosh," I said aloud, thinking of the swamp ducks around Red Rock and the graceless life we lived there. "Beautiful."

"Aren't they?" Ralph looked from me to the swans and back again. We'd brought broken bread and Ralph threw chunks to the swans. When he had their attention he crushed the bread into hard nuggets the size of golf balls and tossed them onto the water where the swans snapped at them greedily.

Ralph laughed. "Yes," he said, "I thought so." He made more bread balls and threw them on the water. He laughed in his sardonic way and half muttered under his breath, "Stuff your faces, you miserable bastards."

"Why did you say that?"

He smirked and gave me a shrug of the shoulders, my shrug. He looked across the pond where a young couple was feeding a pair of mallards. The man threw popcorn through the air to the drake and the woman knelt down and shoveled handfuls at its mate in tentative, underhand motions. "Because," Ralph said, "in this lousy life anything beautiful is also stupid. Bela sed stulta."

There was a moral here I was missing. "And — ?"

"And vice versa . . ." Ralph sighed, expressing weariness I suspected he didn't really feel. "The clever's always ugly."

Later I realized he thought the bread balls he'd thrown to the swans would swell in their bellies and cause them to get stomach cramps, maybe rupture their guts and kill them.

Not everything he did was cruel. On the trolley back to Aunt Ellen's he gave his seat to an old woman who struggled on with parcels, and then at her stop he helped her off, holding up his arm to the driver, traffic-cop style, as she negotiated the steps to the curb. Playing the role of concerned citizen. So there was no pattern. He was as charming or cold-blooded as the mood swings took him. He stole a *Toronto Star* behind the back of a pitiful vendor but he gave two dollars to a hobo who approached us at the trolley stop. He was arbitrary. And pathetic.

What I mean is this. As I watched him flip-flop from one mood to the other I thought those little acts of cruelty were his way of getting back at the world. For what? For making him subject to mood swings that had him singing one minute and sighing the next. For making him less than whole. Unstable. I saw, too, he would stoop to meanness and cruelty to avenge the fact he could never have the peace of mind ordinary people had. Yes, it was pathetic.

When we turned into Aunt Ellen's street he said, "I'll phone the old farts and tell them we're coming home tomorrow."

I gave him one of my younger brother shrugs, pleased by his irreverence. Like I say, he was charming.

"Better yet," he said. "You phone them." He ran his fingers through his hair, roostering it up. "Phone them and say you lost me in the park today. That'll get them going." He cackled and I laughed with him, but not the way we used to when he scared Mother by leaping from behind doors and making her jump. This laughter made me feel hollow inside, like we'd betrayed something important.

Aunt Ellen was resting when we got to the house, so we went upstairs to pack. I sat on the edge of the bed studying my shoes. I saw Ralph had closed up again, but I resolved to speak anyway. To tell him how much I cared for him, the kid brother at last finding the courage to say what he felt in his heart. How much he meant to me, how I loved him. A whole lifetime of unacknowledged gratitudes and affections I had never spoken of before. I wanted to say how much I feared for him, too. The mood swings, the cruelty.

"Before we go, Ralph —"

"Believe me," he interjected, holding up one hand. "I know what you're going to say, kid. And I'm touched . . ." He stood at the dresser sorting through junk we'd accumulated during our stay: city maps, matchbooks, brochures. "I really am."

I paused, waiting for him to say more, summoning my courage again. It was a fateful pause. As the seconds ticked by and I realized he was going to drop it at that, I lost my resolve.

"Look," he said. He had a glossy photo of Lola and the Dancing Damselles of Denmark, and he tossed it across the bed to me. The blonde I'd fallen in love with stood off to Lola's right staring past the camera. Did I say my mouth went dry when I thought of her? My stomach turned inside-out and left me aching with desire. I flipped the photo over in my hands. Across the back Lola had written in round letters: "For Ralph and Dickie, High Rollers from Red Rock."

"I'm not sorry," I said. "What I did."

"Didn't do, you weenie."

"Yes."

"Me neither." Ralph looked at the photo over my shoulder. "Was she — ?"

"Yes," said Ralph, "Beautiful." He snatched the photo from my hand.

"No," I protested. I wanted to keep the photo in my sketchbook and had the crazy notion of pinning it above my desk to look at while I studied. He tore it in pieces and tossed them into the wastebasket along with museum maps and the flyers for downtown restaurants. "Bela sed stulta," he added bitterly.

"No," I whispered. I wanted to say more, to ask Ralph if

it was the blonde he'd gone upstairs with, but couldn't get past the lump in my throat.

Ralph laughed. "Poor Dickie," he said, punching me in the shoulder. "And he didn't even get laid." He snorted. "Mia dika frato."

After a while he said, "I suppose we'd better tell Aunt Ellen we're heading back to that dump of a town."

Twenty-five

Hansi Frudel stood behind the counter at his store and stared blankly. He no longer got any satisfaction ringing up sales on the cash register or surveying what was happening on Main Street. He no longer enjoyed gossiping with the miners as he wrapped their purchases in brown paper. All of that was gone. Once he had carefully selected a clean white shirt for each day of the week, and a tie, but now he arrived at the store some mornings unshaven, wearing a pair of jeans. He was letting himself go. He rarely laughed aloud in the store. He was obsessed with refinancing and walked around in a daze, making calculations in his head. At the cash register, in the stock room, every moment of the day Hansi Frudel was miles away. Who would loan him the money to save the store? Where would he find the collateral?

Gerry Stockton leaned his beefy arms on the counter one day, contemplating Hansi's gloomy face. "My friend," he said, "you look beat."

Hansi nodded agreement. With the boys away in Toronto, he and Tina talked late into the nights: about how much they had in savings, where they would go after Red Rock, what to do with the trust money. They considered each issue from every angle and then rehashed the whole business. The next night they did the same. Most nights there was nothing new to add, but they talked anyway, saying the same things over and over so as not to face the silence. Tina drank strong tea with lumps of sugar, and sometimes splashed in whiskey. She needed its numbing effect before bed. Hansi bought two bottles at the liquor store every Saturday.

"My friend," Gerry said. "You need to get away from here."

Hansi's clouded eyes stared at Gerry. Tall and big-boned, Gerry was gaining weight while Hansi was wasting away: he had taken his belt in two notches. In the past Hansi had felt superior to Gerry because he was independent and Gerry worked nine-to-five for the mine. But recently he'd begun to envy his friend. Having taken few chances, Gerry had little to lose if Red Rock went under. He could pack up and move to the next mining town with no worries. Maybe Gerry was the smarter all along and Hansi had lived in a fool's paradise, believing he was an entrepreneur when he was only a petty shopkeeper.

That's how the world works, Hansi thought. One day you feel superior to a guy like Gerry because he's just a company flunky, and the next you're wishing you were in his shoes.

At least Gerry still came into the store. Where the other miners walked quickly past Hansi's open door and averted their eyes when they met him on the street, Gerry stopped in for a smoke and a talk. His form of solidarity. That showed he was different from the others, a man to whom Hansi could unburden his heart.

Hansi realized he'd been staring out the window. It had been raining for a week. The cars swishing past on the street splashed through puddles and sprayed the display window of Hansi's store. The water ran down in rivulets, leaving red streaks like licorice twists on the glass. Hansi said, "The worst part is the waiting."

"How do you mean?" Gerry lit a cigarette.

"Now I can't make any more payments. Waiting for McGuire to close in. That bloodsucker." Hansi took out his pocketknife and shaved the crown off the nail of his baby finger as he talked.

"You could always sell."

"Sell?"

"Work the whole thing off on someone else. Inventory for sure." Gerry looked around, appraising the store. "The buildings maybe to the company, and the inventory wherever. There's lots of good stuff here."

Inventory, buildings, capital: it sounded simple the way

Gerry said it, but McGuire had tied everything to everything else — stock bought on lines of credit guaranteed through the inventory, inventory coregistered with the buildings, equity in their home serving as collateral. The fact was, nothing could be sold without involving everything else. McGuire had built a house of cards out of Hansi's financial affairs and it was about to collapse as the Red Rock iron mines went under.

"I could sell some of the inventory to Beaver," Hansi offered hopefully. He shaved a little too close with his pocketknife and blood started from the tip of his finger. He didn't seem to notice. "But any monies I realized would go straight to McGuire."

"Then do something else."

Gerry looked at the trickle of blood coming from Hansi's finger. He saw Hansi was already shaving the nail of another finger to the quick. He offered Hansi a cigarette and Hansi lit it with a paper match, which he ground under his toe. Hansi believed cigarettes were filthy and furthermore a crutch. In the army he'd refused to smoke, chewing gum when other men gambled their paycheques for cigarettes, men who begged smokes when theirs ran out. Hansi despised them. He prided himself on his willpower. But now he smoked Gerry's cigarettes to steady his nerves. And he despised himself for it. He wished he could stamp the smoldering match through the floor.

"Do?" asked Hansi. He looked confused. "What?"

There was a long silence while both men puffed and watched the cars gliding by on Main Street.

"There must be something." Gerry picked up his cigarette pack and tucked it into his pocket. "You have to make decisions."

Hansi grunted. In Europe he had made many decisions. There he had stood out. War involved decisions and most men froze when they had to act — men older than him and officers, too, men who hesitated at critical moments, sending soldiers to their graves. Indecision was a weakness Hansi reviled, a cancer working from within people, destroying them eventually. So in Europe he'd always been decisive, even if he endangered his own life. He'd shouted commands, he'd led attacks on machine-gun nests. But now he faced something different. Where his own flesh and blood were concerned Hansi hesitated.

Because the decisions Hansi had to make were not about his own life. They involved Ralph — and now Tina.

Not that Tina made any demands. He knew she'd kept whatever sickness she had from him to spare him, because she would not force him to choose. No, Tina was not making any demands. It was his fear of losing her that ate at him: the girl who'd married him despite his poor prospects, the wife who had suffered to bear their children, nearly died for them. He couldn't imagine a life without Tina, without their long talks into the dark of night. She understood him like no one else. How could he live without someone he depended on so much? How could he choose between her and his son?

If only it didn't mean so much to Ralph. Other men took setbacks like this in stride. He had himself when he was younger. He, too, had been eager to succeed when he was Ralph's age, but he didn't blink when he couldn't go to business school. No. He bounced from one thing to another, confident he would always land on his feet. What was an opportunity passed up here, a missed profit there? Other people took things like that in stride, with a shrug of the shoulders. But not Ralph. With him everything was dramatic, everything was life and death.

Ralph was an odd one, Hansi thought. What sort of person gassed themselves? At one time Hansi believed suicide was the coward's way out, but the look he saw in Ralph's eyes was not cowardice. Despair, yes. And rage, too. Ralph had dreams, and like a child he went blank with rage when he did not get what he wanted. Hansi knew a little about rage himself, so he understood that Ralph was not acting out of cowardice. The other thing he knew was Ralph would try it again. There was no doubt in Hansi's mind.

Hansi looked up suddenly, realizing the cigarette had burned down and was singeing the hair on his knuckles.

Gerry had been talking and he repeated, "You have to decide."

That was easy to say when you weren't faced with the choices yourself, Hansi thought. But how do you choose between wife and son? To give up Hansi's Hardware, into which he had poured all his energy, all his dreams for years, over which he'd fretted and sweated, seemed easy compared to this choice. In his mind the store was already gone: a decade of labor, his pride in ownership, his belief in the capitalist system. Hansi kissed them goodbye. But to choose between Tina and Ralph — as surely he would have to — that he could see no way to do.

Twenty-six

I expected our parents to meet us at the station. From Sudbury west I fidgeted in my seat thinking of them, Father wearing a white shirt, Mother with chocolate bars. I wanted to be back with them — the family, all that. I pestered Ralph about how far we had to go and how long it would take and glanced at my watch when he looked back to his book. It was *Catcher in the Rye*, and he stopped regularly to explain episodes. At one point he bleated "Ducks!" But he didn't explain that.

We sat in a day coach facing each other on bench seats, Ralph sprawled lengthwise with his feet sticking into the aisle, his head propped against the window, straw hair poking up, affecting the look of the blasé traveler.

"This cat Holden Caulfield," he said, talking in the way I imagined the boy in the book did, "really tells people where to get off." Ralph admired that. Putting people in their places.

The train sliced through the Shield. Out the window I saw small lakes with stone bottoms surrounded by bullrushes. Redwinged blackbirds fluttered from stem to stem. Stunted spruces. Swamp ducks. Gravel roads slashing through granite hills. The train slid past tar-paper villages and deserted logging camps and stopped for the grimy mining towns carved out of the rocks and bush. It was all depressingly familiar, the smell, the silence, the sameness. We were getting close to home.

"Hey, Dickie." Ralph waved the book in my face. I returned his grin but did not speak. "How about this guy Caulfield?"

"I don't like all that swearing."

"Li estas la plej granda. La plej fucking granda."

"He's not the greatest. He's a pain."

"He's aces," Ralph said. "He tells girls off, he puts parents and teachers in their place."

"He's too angry, too bitter. He's — crazy."

"You trying to tell me something?"

"I'm talking about a book. Just a character in a book."

Ralph studied me with his cold blue eyes. He snorted.

Time stopped while he took my measure, while I tried to shrug my way out of it, kid brother style. I swear I didn't mean to say it, *crazy*, he was the last person I wanted to hurt — where the word came from I don't know. I stared out the window, I fussed with a smudge on the glass.

Ralph grunted and turned back to his book. Fine red lines mapped his eyes like the capillaries in a drunkard's nose, and there were splotches on his cheeks from late nights, cigars, and alcohol. That cowlick was sticking up on the crown of his skull, the unruly thatch of the mental defective. Again I saw my brother as pathetic. Not nutty and wonderful crazy, but pathetic. He shifted on the seat and continued reading.

I didn't feel so good. I was tired, too. The stress and strain were getting to me. Spying on him, all that. I was as weary as he was agitated, so we were both on edge. Physically drained, nerves raw, we wanted nothing more than the hot tubs, soft beds, and warm food of home. Things we associated with Mother.

The first sign of Red Rock was the garbage dump. Black soot hung in the air. The acrid smell of burning waste. Crows flapped from one swamp spruce to another and squawked at the train. We put our noses to the windows when Ralph spotted a bear shambling into the bush. It disappeared and we were left looking at tin cans, peeling rubber tires, rusting appliances, disintegrating cardboard, moldy food, mattresses with burst stuffing, stacks of papers. Past the dump came the town, nestled in a spruce valley. Then everything was stained red with iron: buildings, cars, streets, faces.

As the train pulled into the station we studied the platform, expecting our parents to be waiting. It was a gray evening, clouds hanging low in the sky.

"No one's here," I said.

"They're hoping we didn't come back." Ralph licked the ends of his fingers and tried to smooth down his hair. I peered up and down the platform. I had bought a silk scarf for Mother and black onyx cufflinks for Father. Where were they?

"Wishful thinking."

We were trying to laugh it off. Ralph swung his bags down. "Bonvena al Red Rock, malgranda frato," he said caustically. We stood for a moment listening to the rumble of blasting from the mines.

I looked for Father's white shirt in the little group on the platform. "I don't get it," I said. "We told them when . . ."

"C'mon," Ralph said. He picked up his bags. "They don't get rid of us that easy."

I clenched and unclenched my fists.

Ralph said, "C'mon. We can't stay on the train."

On the platform we gathered our bags together and looked up and down. There wasn't much of a crowd at the Red Rock station, but we were jostled as families rejoined and a clutch of nuns swirled around jabbering in French. We tried not to look at each other. Ralph spat on the tracks, then went into the station house to check for messages. He returned immediately. He stood beside his bags and shuffled from one foot to the other.

"They forgot us." He raked his hair.

"That's ridiculous," I said. "Let's phone."

"No sirree," he said. "They don't get that satisfaction. Not from this cowboy."

I had the feeling something bad was going to happen and I looked at the sky as if expecting whatever it was to come from the heavens. "We'll get a cab," I said. I dug change out of my pocket.

"The hell with that," Ralph said. "Kaj kun ilin."

Then Father rushed out of the station house. He looked about wildly and bumped into an old woman shuffling along with her bags. He took no notice. His face was flushed and he hadn't shaved. He spotted us and waved one of those big hands. "Here, boys," he shouted over the nuns and pushed past them.

When he came up I smelled whiskey on his breath.

Ralph and I exchanged a glance and then looked at our bags. Something's wrong at the store, I thought.

In all those years of running Hansi's Hardware, good and bad, sales or none, our father never talked business in front of us. It was an unwritten rule around the house that children shouldn't be bothered with adult troubles — money matters, quarrels between Father and Mother, disputes with neighbors, the fate of trust funds. Safe in the cocoon of silence our parents built around us, we experienced little of the suffering of ordinary life. Even when our sister died, we were scuttled to the cemetery as if death were shameful, something you didn't talk about. Only sometimes when things went bad we overheard the strained whisper of conversation from their bedroom late at night. Muffled weeping. Whiskey on Father's breath come morning. We learned to divine from signs when things were not so good between them or at Hansi's Hardware.

So it was natural to think of the store when Father showed up with whiskey on his breath.

He clutched us in a hug and held us for a moment. "Sorry," he said. Then he had our suitcases in his big hands. "Sorry, boys."

He didn't ask about the train, if we had a good time, how we liked Toronto, questions for which I'd prepared answers, oh eager to please and devoted even then to our father. He didn't say why Mother wasn't there. He pointed to the parking lot and started off at a half trot before we'd gathered up our remaining bags.

Ralph looked at me and whispered, "Io estas erara."

"Watch your step," Father called sharply when we came to the wooden stairway. "There's a rotten plank."

We passed by the Rockland Hotel where country music blared out the open windows. Miners in their iron-red boots staggered out of the Men Only door and weaved around the parking lot, shouting and cursing. I expected Father to grunt and deliver a harangue on the manners of miners. Instead he threw our bags unceremoniously into the trunk of the car and slammed it with a bang before hustling us into the seats and closing the doors behind us. Instead we drove silently through town, over the tracks, down Main Street — there was Hansi's Hardware looking the same as ever — and into the garage.

Before we got out Father said, "Boys, there's something I have to tell you." He turned in the driver's seat to look at us. "It's about your mother."

He paused, letting this sink in. "And I expect you to take it like the boys, the men, we're proud to have raised."

Twenty-seven

The worst thing was watching Mother die. Father insisted we go directly to the hospital. In the antiseptic corridors of Red Rock General he said, "It's tough for you boys, but nowhere near as tough as it is for her, so put your best face on." He spoke about strength of character and having backbone — willpower this, manliness that. But he won us over only when he said we owed it to Mother not to show fear because that would weaken her will to fight. We shuddered when he said *leukemia.* We nodded when he instructed us to smile, to show the stoic faces of Frudel defiance: no tears, no breaking down. The manly code according to Hansi Frudel. For Mother we would do anything, even contain our tears.

It sounded easy until we got to the hospital.

On the drive over Father told us what had been happening in Red Rock while we were gone. There was a wildcat strike at the mine. Shrevey Russell's old man got his arm broken in a scuffle. Apparently Bill Russell had parked his car on the road to the mine and refused to let anyone pass. A couple of scabs, toughs from up north hired by the company to bust up the union, had rammed their pickup into his car and jumped down wielding tire irons. Bill Russell had a baseball bat. A crowd gathered, miners on both sides of the dispute, shouting and milling about. Ned Morgan intervened, trying to talk everybody down. But Bill Russell kept shouting "Scabs!" at the toughs until one of them let fly. Broke his arm just below the elbow. The wildcat was still on, but now all the striking miners were armed, some, according to Gerry Stockton, with guns.

Father told us all this as he drove, swinging one arm about for effect as he steered with the other. He was a good story-teller. His big voice carried us past Iver's Diner and the illuminated sign on the mine road reading THIS SITE 40 DAYS WITHOUT A TIME-LOSS INJURY. Father laughed at that. He wiped his brow with a handkerchief. He told the story about the wildcat strike with such good timing Bill Russell was just being carted off to the hospital when we wheeled into its parking lot.

Dr. McGuire stopped us in the hall. Mixed odors of ether and whiskey.

Ralph screwed up his face in mock revulsion and said "Ew" like Patsy Johnson and we laughed into hands capped over our mouths.

With one hand on Father's elbow Dr. McGuire steered him out of earshot and conferred in whispers. While he talked, Father studied the tile floor and picked at a boil under his collar. They stopped talking suddenly and Father rejoined us.

He turned and called after McGuire, "When?"

"The sooner the better." McGuire's voice echoed behind us.

She was sleeping when we entered the room. Head twisted on the pillow, strands of gray hair fallen over one cheek. They fluttered with each breath. I stopped dead in my tracks. I'd never seen her asleep before, it is not something a child sees their mother doing. She was peaceful but helpless. Breathing softly, as though she might slip away at any moment. I knew suddenly the terror of parents watching over their sleeping children, and I uttered a silent prayer having nothing to do with Frudel fortitude, a desperate plea to the Almighty in which I offered my own tawdry life in place of my mother's.

We sat and watched her breathing and twitching.

After a while Father cleared his throat and whispered, "McGuire says sleeping's the best thing for her." He put his hand on my shoulder and squeezed it once. "I need coffee. You boys want some?"

When he was gone I stared at my shoes, waiting for Ralph to speak. He coughed.

"She looks so — so vulnerable," he said.

I asked, "Think she'll die?"

He stood and went to the window. His mood seemed to change when he looked out onto the streets of Red Rock. "Even you'll die someday, Dickie." His back was to me, the rooster tail sticking up.

"It wouldn't be right."

"You mean the parent before the child?"

"I mean *right*. I mean it's wrong for her to die when she wants to live."

"Is there a right and wrong to dying? Cosmic justice?"

"There should be."

"Dikfingro," he said. "Grow up."

I kept my eyes on his back. "She wants to live so much. Look at her." We both stared at her hand, which twitched as she slept, clenching and unclenching the sheet. It was mottled and wasted to the bone. I added cruelly, "She cares."

"So?"

"That's all. It just doesn't seem right." I don't know why I couldn't say the rest — *you don't*. I don't know why I'd said as much as I had.

Ralph snorted and took a step toward me as if he meant to strike me, but instead he turned on his heel and looked at the streets below. Rutted, iron-stained. He asked, "You hate this town, don't you?"

I shrugged.

"Well, I loathe it and everything it stands for. That's no secret. I want to get away from Red Rock and its small-mindedness as badly as anyone's ever wanted to. And because I have a chance everyone thinks I'm a self-centered shit."

He turned to face me. Before he spoke I heard the ticking of electricity in the walls and I thought how awful it would feel to lie there listening to your life tick away.

"I hate this dump with its two-bit code of honor, its stupid pride in mining, its small-town morality, and the transparent hypocrisy it foists on young people — and which they in turn foist on the next generation. You see it, too, don't you, the sham and illusion? Shit, I hate this place." He was running one toe of his sneakers over the tiles, making an irritating squeak. "But I'm scared, Dickie." He butted his fists together. "Just lately I've discovered something else, and it makes me wake up in a sweat."

He closed his eyes and took an audible breath. I couldn't tell whether he was acting, but when he spoke again he fixed me with his brown-spotted eye. "What I've discovered is, there's nothing I don't hate. My friends are parasites, my parents bumbling clowns. Physics is stupid. The arts a con-game. Politics an ass that needs kicking. But here's the most important thing. I discovered I hate myself. I hate myself because I'm a festering pit of ambition, pride, and hatred. Do you know how it feels to hate yourself?"

Though he was whispering, his voice echoed in the little room like struck iron. "Easy," I whispered back. I nodded at Mother.

"You feel there's no point in going on. Ne punkto."

"Don't." I had moved over to the window beside him and I put one hand on his shoulder. We looked at the cars going by in the street, tires caked in iron dust.

Ralph brushed my hand away.

"You, Dickie, are just the opposite. You love." He glanced toward Mother. She stirred, she was waking. Ralph's eyes shifted from the bed to me. "And I don't just mean her. Of course you do love her. And Father, and God knows what else — me probably. Jesus. But most important you love yourself and that makes your life worth living. There's the difference between us. Right there, Dickie. It makes your pathetic life worth living."

There was a sound from the bed and we turned as one.

"Hansi?" Mother raised herself on one elbow. When she saw us she smiled. "Come here, boys," she said, beckoning with her hand.

Her body was a tiny bulge in the bed. Even her fingers seemed shrunk, and her lips collapsed on themselves. She turned her sunken eyes on us and smiled again. How could she have wasted so fast? She motioned us to lean over and kissed us each quickly on the cheek. I felt her lips tremble as they grazed my skin.

"Don't be afraid." She motioned me to the other side of the bed and then took one of each of our hands and lay back on the pillows. She whispered, "Help your father around the house. The laundry, the cooking, Thursday is garbage day." She closed her eyes and breathed softly.

And when Father returned she smiled again. "You brought tea," she said, pleased in a schoolgirl way. She took the mug. "I'm so glad it's Mint and not that dishwater Pekoe they bring at breakfast."

When she drank, bubbles of saliva formed in the corners of her mouth. Father stooped over her slight figure and wiped them away with a handkerchief. "Too hot?" he asked. He sat beside the bed with his hand on her arm. Tears bulged the corners of his eyes but he choked them back.

She smiled at us over his head. "Just right." She sipped a few times, then lay back in the pillows with a sigh.

It was astounding how quickly she was out again, blue-veined wrists turned up, mouth fallen open. Father pointed us to the door, and we slipped out like thieves in the night.

In the car he turned to us before he started away. His face was ashen and his lips trembled. "McGuire says she has to go away."

"Away?" I thought this was a euphemism and recoiled with horror. I repeated, "Go away? Where?"

Father started the engine and pulled into the street. "To Rochester," he said over his shoulder. "Where they do blood transfusions and operations on bone marrow. McGuire says we have no other choice. And it's worked, they've saved lives." He took out his handkerchief and blew his nose.

"The Richter-Lebrun process," Ralph said. He choked the words out and I thought he was going to cry, too.

"The what?" I asked.

Ralph pushed one hand through his hair. He hissed through clenched teeth, "It costs piles. It costs piles of money."

Father stopped at an intersection. "Only it's awful expensive," he continued as if he hadn't heard. "You know?" He tried to look at us both but his eyes dodged away from Ralph's and settled on mine. He drove a few blocks and we listened to the rumble of tires and watched iron dust swirl in the streets.

Then Father pulled the car onto the shoulder. He banged his fists on the steering wheel. "God damn," he shouted. He banged his fists on the wheel again and again.

Twenty-eight

That's probably when Ralph made up his mind. Certainly he wasn't the type to stand by debating pros and cons when he felt angry. For somebody with a reputation as a thinker he was dangerously emotional. While we sat there in the car, Father bent over the wheel, Ralph pressed his thumbs against his temples until his arms began to shake. When he put them down there were circles the size of quarters on his temples, blue-white.

Father pulled himself together and wheeled back onto the street. I picked at loose threads on the carseat. The Meteor was getting old. Ralph stared out the window, rubbing his temples from time to time.

"By gum," Father said, "I bet you boys are hungry." He was trying to gloss things over with his big voice, with brittle but forced enthusiasm. "I feel the same myself. I feel like one of Iver's big nips with lots of onions." He looked into the back seat. "And a Pepsi."

He gunned the motor. He took the corner onto Main Street too fast and the tires squealed. "It's either that," he said, "or a dose of my scrambled eggs."

He laughed and I chuckled along with him, thinking of the meals he'd made whenever Mother was unable to. Whatever Father had learned in the days when he operated Hansi's Hot Foods it was not how to cook. Ralph shot a sharp look at me and went back to staring out the window. In the falling light his eyes looked washed-out, but determination was knit on his brow.

At Iver's, Father left us together when he went to place our order.

"You make me puke." Ralph spoke without looking at me. "Vomema," he repeated.

"For trying to make it easier on him?"

"For sucking up to him like a five-year-old. For letting him think he's done the right thing."

"He has done the right thing."

"You see."

I picked at the carseat. "I just want to help."

"You want to make it easy on yourself." Ralph spoke between his teeth. "For a tub of lard," he said, "you're a gutless goddamn wonder."

There were times I wanted to smash his face in, but I never did. "Call it what you will." The thread I was picking at unraveled suddenly with a ripping sound and came away in my hand.

Ralph snorted. "Get a load of him up there jawing with that fascist Iver. One capitalist swine to another. Going over the economic climate and the prospects for growth in this quarter."

Ralph spat out the window.

"Would you guess he had a wife dying in the hospital? That his family's cracking up?"

"Not everyone's cracking up."

"That's what I like about you, Dickie." Ralph spun on me. "You've inherited a nice sense of self-righteousness. You've got so much Frudel piety you stink with it. Vi odoracas."

"I don't wallow in self-pity."

"Congratulations," Ralph said. "But take a close look, Dickie my boy, and you may wish you did. Because that's you up there yukking it up with Iver while your wife lies dying."

Ralph stared out the windshield, then turned to me again as if he'd just thought of something. "You know, you're as close to Hansi Frudel as it gets. The buffoon running a two-bit business using fifty-dollar words to back up a bankrupt morality. That's you, Dickie my boy, the big mouth full of nothing but hot air."

I turned away, unable even to shrug.

Later that night when Father was at the hospital Ralph

called me into his room. "Heartbreak Hotel" was on the phonograph. Papers lay about the floor. On one corner of his desk stood an open bottle of whiskey and a water glass. Ralph had another in his hand. "Join the party," he said. He splashed whiskey into the tumbler and passed it to me. "Bottoms up." He watched as I raised the glass to my lips. His eyes were glazed and that cowlick would have looked comic if there was anything at all humorous in the scene.

I gulped a mouthful and gagged. "What is it?"

"Jim Beam." Ralph took a mouthful. "Want some Coke?"

"This tastes awful."

"It's supposed to."

"Taste like shit?"

"Don't you understand anything, Dickie? Life is eating a lot of shit. This stuff gets you used to it. Call it an acquired taste."

Ralph refilled his glass and sat on the edge of the bed. "A toast. To Frudel fortitude." He held up his glass in mock salute. "The legacy of Hansi." He added, "To Frudel guts and taking it like a man." When he drank whiskey ran past his mouth and dribbled onto his shirt, but he didn't notice. He produced a cigar from the desk drawer and lit it. When the flame took, he stood in the center of the room, glass in one hand, smoldering stogie in the other. He pointed the stogie at me. "Hey," he said. "Drink up, little brother."

I took another swallow even though I had no taste for it. For perhaps the first time I wanted to be well away from Ralph and his mad eyes. The manic force that went into turning a room upside down and stealing liquor from Father's cabinet and dragging me into his demented world. His obsessions.

"Another toast." Ralph clinked my glass. "This time to Werner von Braun and the wonders of science." Ralph took all the whiskey in a gulp and smashed his tumbler against the wall. "That fascist swine."

"I need some water." I turned to go.

"Oh no you don't." Ralph's hand seized my shoulder. A small but powerful grip digging into my flesh. A passionate grip, which even with my linebacker's bulk I could not shake.

143

He produced another glass from the rubble on his desk and poured into it. "Here." He splashed bourbon into my glass and said, "As often as you do this in remembrance of me." He laughed in his superior way and asked with mock concern, "Do I offend you with sacrilege? My God-fearing kid brother?"

"No."

"You think I'm crazy."

"I think you're pathetic."

"Good." He clinked glasses again. "That shows a little spine in you." He drained off the whiskey and went to the bottle at the desk. He paused as if suddenly remembering something. "But I didn't ask you here to exchange pleasantries. Oh no. I had something else in mind." He placed the cigar on the edge of the desk, making sure it wouldn't fall to the floor. "This meeting is for your benefit." He dug around in the jumbled bed clothes. He turned so as to shield what was concealed there from me and added, "Your edification."

He produced a Luger. Father's. A souvenir from his war trunk. I had seen it only once before but I recognized it instantly. How it came into Ralph's possession was a mystery, because Father kept his war trunk as safely locked away as the memories of what had happened to him in Italy — deaths he'd seen, deaths he'd caused.

"It's a fine piece." Ralph held it up to the light for me to see. He was right. It was a beautiful gun, made of blue-black metal with a swastika stamped into the handle. He worked the action. The clicking and snapping of metal echoed in the room like gun shots.

"Look, Dickie," he went on, "precision German craftsmanship. Manufactured perhaps in the very town from which the Frudels emigrated lo so many years ago. Those DPs. You appreciate the symmetry?" He smirked. "Then consider this, Dickie my boy, my blundering brother. Perhaps this very piece was manufactured by Werner von Braun himself. Or one of his fascist relatives."

He stuck the barrel into his mouth and when I gasped he pulled it out, laughing.

144

Then he jammed the pistol down the front of his trousers the way thugs did in movies and poured more whiskey. His words slurred when he said, "Here's the point, Dickie." From a pocket he produced two shells. Short and liquor-bright, they were nestled in his palm but looked to me the size of railroad spikes. "You'll enjoy the mystery," he said. "You'll appreciate this symmetry. One's for me. That much is easy to figure out, yes? That much we understand right away. La mistero estas, Dickie my devoted kid brother, trusted son and confidant, la mistero estas, who's the other one for? Kiu?"

Twenty-nine

Though sweat ran down my broad back and my knees knocked, I was certain the second bright shell wasn't for me. How could it be? To Ralph I was nothing — at most a butt for his cruel remarks, a target. Less important than strangers he met on the street or kids he quarreled with at school. I was poor Dickie, unworthy even of my brother's anger. He made it obvious by telling me what he was going to do and then laughing in my face.

"Look," he said, pointing to the smoke rings he blew at the ceiling. He lay on the bed now, Luger in his lap, the neck of the whiskey bottle grasped in one hand. I stood near the door, wanting to bolt. His brown-spotted eye twitched from my face to the smoke rings to his book shelves. Most of the books were scattered on the floor, face down. Some had pages ripped out. "Stulta Dickie," he crooned. He waved the Luger in a circle and then pointed it at my midsection. "Mia stulta dika frato." He smirked, challenging me to step across the room, to struggle for the pistol, to do anything but shrug it off, the perpetual good loser.

I'd been standing with my hands in my pockets. I took them out and examined them. They were big as hams, but not the hands of a fighter or a killer. Even if I had wanted to strangle him, I could not have done it. I bolted.

I left him swigging bourbon and jeering my cowardice. I dumped the dregs of my drink in the kitchen sink and rinsed the tumbler clean of tell-tale residues.

For one moment I hesitated. I studied my face in the window over the sink, knowing I was abandoning him. The thought sickened me. He was capable of anything, yet I was not going to stop him.

I was done with all that — with worrying about setbacks and pistols, and betrayals and razor blades. With cream-colored envelopes from Werner von Braun. Even a devoted kid brother could ride the roller coaster of Ralph's emotions only so long. I was exhausted and beginning to lose my grip. There were moments when I contemplated the suicides of my cousins with something akin to relief — and I had to shut my mind to tempting images of deep rivers and cool shotguns.

When I bolted from Ralph's room I had no plan in mind. I suppose I intended to hang around outside the house and intercept Father returning from Red Rock General. There was no question of telling him about the whiskey or the Luger; I was a coward but would not stoop to snitching. So I balanced my loyalties. I wanted to make sure Father didn't come across Ralph in that psychotic state — and with a loaded gun. He needed protection. But so did Ralph — because God knows what might happen if those two came upon each other in their separate moods of desperation.

I suppose, too, I hoped Father would stay away long enough for the whiskey to wear off and for Ralph to regain his senses. The old pendulum swing. If enough time passed he'd escape his demons, as he always had before — always with one exception — then free from the crush of alcohol, he'd put the Luger back and forget all about bright bullets and black intentions. Yes, I hoped for that.

There was no doubt in my mind who the second shell was meant for. When Ralph spit out Father's name, *Hansi*, goose bumps rose on my flesh. What accounted for such loathing? We agreed Father's idea of capitalism amounted to little more than bourgeois pretensions, that he was no more than a small-time money-grubber. But Ralph's hate seemed out of proportion to that. No, it had to do with failure. With the fact Father hadn't lived up to his cherished capitalist slogans: profits especially. He'd failed to acquire the wealth and power of money grubbing. The money, in short, to send

Ralph to Cal Tech. Yes, that was it. So Ralph hated him for failing, and doubly for loving Mother too much. For the fact Father was prepared to consign the wunderkind to the dustbin of science forever.

At least Ralph saw it in those dramatic terms: betrayal, defeat. His mind worked that way, exaggerating things so minor setbacks became major catastrophes. So where I would have shrugged off the loss of the trust and waited for another day, where anyone else would have put the needs of their dying mother first, Ralph came apart when it became obvious the trust money would be used to send Mother to Rochester for medical treatments and not for his tuition to Cal Tech. Utterly undone. And maybe he was not to be judged too severely for that. Because the fixation was beyond his control, it overwhelmed those sensible voices that in other people cry out for compassion and patience and self-denial. It made him see Father as a monster, since he could not blame our dying mother — who could?

That, anyway, was how I saw it.

Near the bottom of the yard Father had placed a wooden bench where we sat on summer evenings, enjoying the mild air and the quiet. I found myself there in the gathering gloom, picking at splinters in the wood and watching the shadows of spruces dance on the grass at my feet. The light still shone from Ralph's room, and from time to time a silhouette crossed the window. It seemed hours since I'd left him. Maybe he'd put away the Luger. I hoped. Maybe it was just a bad joke Ralph would laugh off in the morning. There was a time when that happened, when Ralph burst out of depressions with a cackle, when he made jokes about my square clothes and strutted around in his T-shirt, doing his hardrock impression. No longer.

The rumble of Euclids working the night shift at the mines echoed in the still air. An owl hooted in the trees behind me, and when I stood in fright, it flapped over the house in the direction of the school.

I saw someone moving toward me from the side of the house. Sweat streamed from my armpits. Was it Ralph? Was he carrying the Luger? I considered a route of escape, and while my mind jumped from one possibility to another I saw it was only Father, who'd parked the Meteor on the street and stepped into the yard for a breath of air after the hospital.

At first he didn't see me, and he stood with his hands on his hips looking at the stars.

Thinking I might intrude on a private moment, I coughed and sat down.

"Dickie." Father seemed surprised to find me there. He told me once he had taken to studying the constellations when he was soldiering in Italy. They comforted him in a world gone crazy, where nothing meant what it once seemed to and no one could be relied on. The stars were constant and fixed.

"An owl hooted in the trees." My mouth was dry and my voice quivered. "You just missed it."

"It flew over my head." He sat beside me on the bench.

"Scared me half to death."

"They'll do that." He laughed, snorted under his breath, really. "Your grandmother thought they were omens."

We considered this for a moment. Grandmother claimed a black cat crossing your path meant bad luck, a loose thread on your clothing meant bad news. I didn't know about owls.

Father added, "Don't worry. It's just superstition." I nodded and we thought our private thoughts while we considered the stars. I felt his hand on my shoulder. "It takes more than a night bird to frighten us Frudels, eh?"

There was so much about him I loved. His hand on my shoulder gave me strength. His voice lay down chunks of solid sound you could trust — at the end of a night filled with shifting shadows and unspeakable fears. All I wanted was to sit there in the gathering dark and be close to my father. It seemed a small thing for a younger brother to ask. All I wanted was to lose myself in the sounds of deepening night.

Thirty

He might have warned us with a cry, a warning shot. But it was not like Ralph to give warnings.

It was peaceful sitting in the dark with the stars blinking overhead, the spruces shushing in the breeze. I've always found trees comforting — even in Queen's Park. You sit down. You keep still. After a while the trees start whispering to you. They have quiet voices. And there was Father's voice, too. Bathed in his calm breathing, I willed the night to slip past, I wished away all the bad things I imagined happening.

He might have turned off the light in his room or drawn the curtains suddenly. Something to attract attention. But that was not like Ralph either. Always one step ahead, always drawing attention to how clever he was. Or desperate.

It seemed hours passed out there. Father talked about the constellations. He tried to help me find Orion, pointing, and when I couldn't we settled on the Big Dipper. Neither of us made a move to go inside. Neither of us even spoke his name. The fact is, we both wanted to hide and not only in the shadows of trees.

Father told me about something that had happened in Europe, about an Italian peasant who didn't want to lose his sons when the fascists were conscripting teenagers, a noble man, according to Father. I nodded in the dark, grunting at appropriate places to let him know I appreciated the story's moral.

"It was a simple thing," Father said, "yet an important one, too, because the man made a choice. You see?" He left a silence but neither of us expected me to answer. There was a spell over us as we sat there on the bench, removed from time, removed from cares and concerns.

"The point lies," Father said, "in what the peasant did, not the way things turned out." He paused to loosen the collar of his shirt.

He had explained how the peasant had hidden his sons in a hole under his barn to keep them from the fascists during the last months of the war. The boys had to stay there longer than their father had figured — they'd suffocated to death.

There was whiskey on Father's breath, not the raw fumes of drunkenness, but the pleasant scent a boy associates with his father and night-time kisses. Midnight aftershave. "And the point isn't that you or I would make the same choice. The point is he made it when he had to."

Father was certain of that and he sealed his certainty with a sigh. Everything was as clear as the stars to Father. He knew what was good and what was bad, and he knew when called on I would do the right thing. He told me so. It was a world of black and white choices he outlined for me there in the shadow of the spruces, a world I wanted to believe in, pushed and pulled as I was by our family worries — Mother's sickness, Ralph's despair, Father's endless brooding over money. "Never forget this," he said. "It doesn't matter what happens in the end if your intentions are honorable."

I wanted to ask him about that, about honorable intentions. I sensed he was in a mood for confidences and suddenly I felt the need to tell him about the day at school when Shrevey Russell called him a Nazi and Ralph and I sprang to his defense. There was an example he would appreciate. I wanted to tell him about that. "Dad," I began, and he looked at me as if he understood how long I'd been waiting to speak.

"Yes, son," he said.

It was then we heard the shot.

I leapt up, stumbling over the bench. I turned to Father, who hadn't moved. I expected him to be on his feet, the man of action, I expected him to be racing to the rescue, like Audie Murphy and G. I. Joe. Instead he groaned as if he'd expected that shot all along and now was forced to deal with it against his will. The groan of a tired man who's looking for a way out.

But there was no way out.

We ran for the house. The dew on the grass was heavy and I slipped. At the back door Father fumbled with the latch and swore under his breath. When we entered the hallway I suddenly remembered Ralph's taunts about the second bullet and my hair stood on end. I saw Father running blind through the door toward the barrel of the smoking Luger, I saw Ralph's laughing face, Father spinning helpless from the impact of the bullet while blood trickled from his mouth. I tried to call out, but my tongue stuck in my throat. Father with a hole in his back the size of a baseball pirouetted in slow motion and looked back at me, accusing.

What happened was much less dramatic: Father crouched at the door to Ralph's room for a moment and looked about quickly. From behind I saw his shoulders sag suddenly and I thought I heard him sigh. He motioned me to move forward. That, too, was a surprise. I expected he'd hold me back from whatever hideous sight awaited us. He'd always done so before, protecting Ralph and me from the ugliness of life.

"Come here," he said. His big hand beckoned. "Come here and see, son." There was sadness in his voice. And defeat.

I don't know why he did that. Perhaps he knew we'd been protected from life's ugliness too long — the violence, the adultery, the sordid mayhem of life in Red Rock. The time for sheltering had passed. Though it was not cruelty I saw in his eyes but tenderness. A kind of apology. Or perhaps it was the final lesson: What to Do When Your Brother Blows His Brains Out.

What I saw had nothing to do with despair or betrayal. The pain of setbacks. It wasn't even human. The acrid odor of burnt cordite filled the small room. Smells of blood and excrement. In an instant my face broke into sweat and my insides revolted. I tottered into the bathroom and knelt with the cold porcelain to my forehead. My mind was blank. I could not even pray.

It was not unusual for boys raised in Red Rock to see death close up. Afternoons in the summer we roamed the granite hills with guns. Small-caliber rifles mostly, .22s and so on, with which we murdered spruce grouse pecking stones on abandoned logging paths. Sometimes we winged blackbirds unlucky enough to draw our attention with their raucous calls. We were cruel in the way of boys, killing slowly and with the attention to detail of the curious. But our weapons were small, our victims unimportant.

The effect of a large-bore pistol discharged close to a human head was remarkable. Even Father, who'd witnessed slaughter first hand, vomited in the kitchen sink. At first it sounded as if he was crying.

After a while I heard him muttering, "Hansi, Hansi, Hansi." Then the scraping of chairs on the kitchen floor. I heard the clink of a bottle against a tumbler, more vomiting, and then silence. After a while the cold porcelain of the toilet bowl cleared my head. The throbbing subsided. I heard the buzz of the electric clock and the refrigerator humming.

I drank cold water and tried to wash the taste of death from my mouth. I looked in the mirror over the sink and saw a face I did not recognize — ashen, yes, but older somehow, too. The house was silent.

In the kitchen Father had poured a tumbler of whiskey for me and pushed a chair back at the table. "Drink," he said. He pushed the tumbler toward me, but not the piece of paper he was reading. It was a note in Ralph's hand, neat tiny writing, like the solution to a problem in math. Words, though, and not many. I knew what it said and I did not want to read it.

Father loosened his tie and rolled up his sleeves. He had the distracted look in his eyes of someone close to death. "How stupid," he said. "How utterly senseless." He groaned and took a gulp of whiskey. He looked at me but I don't think he really saw me. He was rambling, phrases came from his mouth without connection: *Belsen, Dachau, egotism.* He studied me over the lip of his glass. "Just a waste," he said finally. "Just a stupid waste."

I thought he was talking about Ralph.

Thirty-one

Later they said Hansi Frudel was drunk and out of his mind with grief, so that explained what he did.

The evidence was this: he'd finished off the Jim Beam before getting up from the table because when the police chief arrived the empty bottle stood on the kitchen counter. The table had been wiped clean and the chairs pushed back into place. The chief also found a crumpled cigarette pack in the trash can and an ashtray with two butts.

The police chief was Dougald Duncan, a retired army captain and veteran of the same European campaign as Hansi. He walked with a limp. When Hansi arrived at the police station it was past 2 a.m. on the clock, and Duncan assumed he'd come in to report a road accident. Hansi's knuckles, he wrote in his little notebook were bloody, his white shirt soiled, his hair rumpled.

Hansi sat across from Duncan and mopped his brow with the polka-dot handkerchief he carried in a back pocket. Being old friends, they dispensed with formalities. Hansi complained about the rash he'd picked up in Italy. He asked Duncan for a glass of water. "I'm burning up in here," he said, tapping his chest with a blood-stained finger. When Duncan limped back from the washroom with the water, Hansi took one sip, placed the tumbler on the desk between them, and then forgot about it while they talked.

Duncan was struck by the way Hansi told his story, recounting the night's events in the third person, as if they had happened to someone else. It confused the police chief at first. One of Hansi's statements that Duncan wrote down concerned Ralph's body: "They discovered the bloody corpse in the back bedroom." It was one of the things Duncan had difficulty understanding. He assumed there'd been a highway accident, so it took him a while to get that notion out of his head. And Hansi's odd way of saying things confused him further. It appeared, Duncan said later, that Hansi wanted to take the point of view of someone no longer associated with the events, of someone who wanted nothing to do with them.

Hansi kept coming back to the gun, the Luger. He kept it as a remembrance of a Wehrmacht soldier he'd encountered in 1945, Hansi explained to Duncan. He wasn't usually a sentimental man, but this was different. The German soldier was a sniper captured by Canadian troops in the last days of the war, and his life was spared by the officer in charge — Hansi. As thanks the soldier offered Hansi everything he was carrying on him: money, chocolate bars, a family ring, trivial things meaning everything to a soldier far from home. Hansi was touched by the gesture. He let the soldier keep his food and his family mementos, but he took the Luger to remind himself of a day when he opened his heart to another human being. He told all this to Duncan in a halting voice. Now a dozen years later the gun had killed his son. He blamed himself that his sentiments as a soldier had put the weapon into Ralph's desperate hands.

Chief Duncan was more concerned about facts. "Did you move the body?" He was pulling on his leather jacket when he asked this.

Hansi seemed not to hear him. "Senseless," he muttered.

"And the other boy's at home?"

"In the back bedroom," Hansi said.

"I'll drive you."

Hansi stood abruptly, refusing the ride. He knocked over the water glass as he did, soaking his foot. He studied it as if seeing it for the first time. He blurted, "I have to go now." He bolted out the door. Duncan wondered about the way he left so suddenly and blamed himself for what happened later.

By the time Duncan had locked up the police station the rear lights of Hansi's Meteor were gone. Duncan cursed night duty, the fact there was only one officer at the station. He should have stayed close to Hansi. He was clearly agitated and that was never a good sign. Duncan drove across town as quickly as he could.

At the house he waited in the cruiser for some minutes, wondering why Hansi was taking so long to get there. He made notes in his little book. Then he cursed himself for waiting. He stumped up the front steps. The front door was locked, but the back door was swinging open. On the kitchen counter he noted the whiskey bottle, the chairs, the ashtray.

He stopped in the hallway. He recalled Hansi saying something about a back bedroom. He considered calling out but thought better of it. Instead he put his hand on the butt of his service revolver and reminded himself he was retiring in two years. The time for foolish chances was long past.

When he came out of the bedroom he sat at the kitchen table with a tumbler of water and listened to the sounds of the early morning: birds, breezes, the occasional motor. He held the tumbler against his cheek and felt its coolness and thought about the violent deaths he'd seen. His sergeant was cut down in Italy as they ran up a road together, his head going one way, his body the other, but that was in the heat of battle. It was his first experience of violent death, though, and it had stayed with him. After that he saw many men die. But none had looked like this.

He waited for ten minutes before calling the coroner, Andrew McGuire. And then he called an undertaker. The clock over the refrigerator read 3:30. He knew Hansi Frudel was not coming home, and when Dr. McGuire arrived, he took the cruiser out on the streets, looking for the Meteor.

First he checked the back alleys and then the deserted parking lots. If he found the Meteor in one of these places there was still hope. He'd find a drunk in a stupor: crying, raging, incoherent, but still alive. Every night someone was hurting and the pattern their pain took was predictable, if the people were not. One night it had been a dentist whose wife had run off with a miner: the drunk dentist had threatened to throw himself off a drag line at the mine and it had taken

156

hours to talk him down. Another time a widow with three children brandished a gun until she broke down, sobbing, and threw the pistol impotently onto the floor. Dramatics. Fear made people irrational — fear and guilt.

When he'd checked the alleys and parking lots he headed for the treacherous spots on the highway, the accident spots. At least there hadn't been a note. That was the fateful tip-off. He'd looked for it on the kitchen table, or somewhere grotesquely conspicuous, pinned to the body of the boy, maybe. Duncan had seen that once. He marveled at the monstrosities ordinary people were capable of, the things he'd seen and couldn't tell anyone.

Around 4:30 he began on the highway, and the first place he drove to was Dead-Man's Curve. Three miles out of Red Rock, it was the site of scores of deaths and hundreds of near misses. At least one car of drunk teenagers drove into the rock-facing of Dead-Man's Curve every summer. It was also a good place to do yourself in. But Duncan doubted Hansi would pick Dead-Man's Curve. It was too predictable for a man like Hansi.

He drove past slowly and stopped the cruiser a hundred yards beyond the curve. The ditches were deep and sometimes cars were hidden from the highway in the bullrushes and scrub willows. His flashlight picked out a skunk in the gravel verge and the startled eyes of a moose feeding in the grass.

The Meteor was at the next curve, two long swerving gouges in the gravel indicated braking before impact into a wall of sheer granite. The passenger's door had sprung open. Steam hissed from the punctured radiator. To be braking that way and yet be crushed like an accordion the car had to be doing at least eighty.

On the seat beside Hansi was an open bottle of whiskey, surprisingly not broken. The only hitch was Hansi's right foot was still pressed on the accelerator pedal. But that was between Duncan and his conscience. Hansi's family had gone through enough without being denied the insurance money. Even before he took out his little book Duncan knew the phrases he would write: *fatal highway accident, distraught driver, dangerous curve,* but no mention of alcohol.

He bent over Hansi's body and tipped the head back in his hand. Yes, the eyes were still open. That was Hansi all over, Duncan thought, looking death in the face. He closed them with his fingers and laid the body out straight on the carseat. In the cruiser he carried a gray wool blanket, and when he'd collected it he stumped back to throw it over Hansi's body.

Then he wrote his report.

Thirty-two

Mother survived. Five-foot-four and graying, a little soft around the middle, she was the tough nut in the family, the one with the Frudel fortitude. After that first bout in Red Rock General, Dr. McGuire arranged a place for her at the Rochester clinic where they did the blood transfusions. I know metastatic tissue had something to do with her case, but I cannot recall whether that is the thing Mother nearly died of or the reaction of her system that saved her life. In any case, the transfusions proved successful. In six months she was back in her own bed, sipping Earl Grey and reading movie magazines. Evenings we drank Cointreau with our tea, sometimes Benedictine, but never whiskey.

Her routine was simple: rest in the mornings, eat several small meals through the day, take a walk in the fresh air before bed.

I was her nurse. Mornings I made toast, soups for lunch, light snacks in the afternoon. We listened to The Happy Gang some days but they seemed too consciously bubbly for our taste, so we tuned in the country station instead. It played the sad songs we identified with in those days. My skills in the kitchen flourished. I made omelettes — tomatoes, cheese, and mushroom, which Mother claimed were nothing less than spectacular.

She spent a lot of time alone. I checked in on her throughout the day, fetching magazines, helping tune the television, which I'd moved to the foot of her bed — ever the dutiful son. I learned about making tea: in those days she drank Licorice and Peppermint. Sometimes we just sat and talked. I had the impression she was surprised to be alive and determined to take advantage of every day. And like me, she was grateful for the family she had left.

Sometimes she looked up from "Queen for a Day" when I puttered at some chore in the room and said, "Come here." And I sat by the bed holding her hand or stroking her forehead as we chatted. We did not shy away from sentiment.

She never talked about Ralph. When goings-on at school were our topic of conversation, we steered clear of his name. I do not think she blamed him for what had happened. With so many bodies in the ground we were beyond blame and blaming.

There were times I came into the bedroom and found her looking through photo albums. She liked the pictures of her wedding, Hansi in his army uniform, flanked by a smiling girl in a splendid white dress hardly recognizable as herself — a girl wearing her hair in ringlets under a flat box hat. She had a lovely smile, innocent. She also liked shots of the four of us on picnics, Ralph cavorting in the background and the dutiful younger son sitting between his parents on the grass in a striped beach shirt. In those photos I was the one with the shock of blond hair roostering up on my head.

One day when I brought the afternoon tea she said, "It's time I got on my feet again." And for the next week we stumbled into each other around the kitchen before she reclaimed her territory, banishing me to the dining room where she could talk to me but not have me underfoot.

Then she announced one day, "I'm buying the house back from the bank" — the money coming from Father's life insurance, but neither of us mentioned that. On another day she said, "This wallpaper's ten years old. What do you think of putting up new stuff?" We sat in the living room for several nights going through catalogues, a pot of tea nearby. "What about this?" she asked, pointing at patterns of red and white circles. She flipped a page. "Do you prefer vertical or horizontal stripes?" I confess I shrugged and tried to slip away.

She needed more than a change of wallpaper. Painful reminders were everywhere. The Toronto-Dominion had taken over the hardware, but the neon sign still flashed HANSI'S up and down Main Street.

I avoided going downtown. I spent a lot of time around the house. Mother stopped shopping at the Safeway next door to the hardware. But she couldn't avoid bumping into people on the streets of Red Rock: Badger Mendez, Mrs. Prungle, Dr. McGuire, the Dobson kids. Staying in Red Rock meant a life of sudden and painful memories.

So then I said, "Why not sell the house?"

"Sell?"

"So you could move out of Red Rock."

"But Red Rock's your home."

"Not after all this." I waved my arm around as if that explained my meaning. "I just want to get out." I longed to say Red Rock was a dying town and a place of death, but that was Ralph's kind of cruelty, and anyway we both knew what I meant.

She went around the house for a few days afterwards running her fingers absently along the oak woodwork and staring blankly out windows. I think she'd believed we could make a home there. Or felt guilty about abandoning the house Hansi had built with his own hands, the house her family had grown up in. Then I saw her leafing through investment pamphlets and scratching numbers on pads while she sipped evening tea. I kept my distance.

One night she showed me the papers returning the house to the bank. There was some good in McGuire: he'd bought the place back for the same price she'd paid the bank.

I nodded. "Now what?" We were sitting at the dining-room table with a pot of tea and a bottle of Cointreau.

"Goodbye, Red Rock." She spoke in a flip way, reminding me of Ralph at his most engaging, his most charming, and I heard his voice add in Esperanto, *Red Rock, adiau!*

"And go where?"

"Wherever you want." She looked me in the eye. "There's your education to think of. Your future."

"No," I said, "I'm done with school." It took all my strength not to shrug and let things ride. But I screwed up my courage. "I'm done with books and teachers and Shrevey Russells."

We sat through a long silence, sipping tea, not looking at each other.

"Then we can live with your great-aunt in Winnipeg."

"I'm going to Toronto."

I'm not sure how that came out but it was clear by the tone that I meant it. Mother raised her eyebrows. We sat through another long silence while we mulled things over: what we had lost, how we had finally come to know each other in sorrow, how we trusted each other now, what it would mean to live in cities thousands of miles from each other.

She placed her thin hand on my wrist. "Good," she said. She smiled in a way I'd become accustomed to since she'd returned from Rochester, a way acknowledging me and the decisions I made for myself. And I recognized in her a goodness that had been suppressed through all the years of being Hansi's wife and our mother. A wonderful capacity to give. Warmth. Trust. I realized what a difficult man Hansi had been to live with, how he had dominated the house. And how he must have forced on her the role of caring mother as he'd insisted upon dutiful sons for us.

I went around the table and kissed her on the cheek. It was the first time I'd kissed her since I was a child in knee pants, and I felt something behind my heart suddenly lift.

She put her hand on my cheek and whispered, "You just do that."

I went back to my chair. We sat looking at each other over our tea, smiling and talking about the future. At one point we both started to laugh, chuckle really. She wanted to know everything about Toronto. Where I would live, what I planned to do. How I'd spend the money she'd send me. I hadn't thought any of this through, but I made it up as I went along.

At first she couldn't believe I wanted to be a writer, but then she said, "Yes. Do exactly what you want with your life. Have a dream and live it."

It was then, I think, she determined on adopting the girl, though she must have been considering it for some time. A baby when she first brought her home, with black hair and big gray eyes. There was nothing of the wildness I recall in Ralph's, or the uncertainty in my own: only the wonder I'd seen in Mother when she first announced she was going to adopt. A gorgeous baby girl with pudgy arms and a high laugh.

They lived for a while with Great-Aunt Helen, but after Mother opened Tina's Teas, a specialty shop in Osborne Village, they moved into the apartment directly above. Sally, my mother called her little girl.

Sally was five last month, and if I read Mother's letter correctly, shows an aptitude for music and painting, but absolutely none whatever — I heard Mother's sigh over the two thousand miles — for math or physics.